FRANCIS DURBRIDGE

Paul Temple Intervenes

COLLINS
CRIME
CLUB

COLLINS CRIME CLUB

An imprint of HarperCollinsPublishers
1 London Bridge Street
London SE1 9GF
www.harpercollins.co.uk

This paperback edition 2015

First published in Great Britain by
LONG 1944

A catalogue record for this book is
available from the British Library

ISBN 978-0-00-812562-2

Set in Sabon by Born Group using Atomik ePublisher from Easypress

MIX
Paper from
responsible sources
FSC™ C007454

CONTENTS

CHAPTER I

On the Air

PAUL TEMPLE never failed to extract the utmost enjoyment from a trip to America; the inconceivable vastness of the continent with its astonishing gamut of civilisations appealed to his sensitive imagination. He was forever planning a novel of some considerable length dealing with the adventures of an Englishman in search of the hidden powers behind American life. So far, it was just an idea, just recognisable in the half-dozen random jottings in the notebook he invariably carried. And at the moment there did not seem to be much possibility of its materialisation into any substantial form. For Paul Temple was very busy indeed on his present trip to the United States.

It had started with an abrupt summons from Colonel Randall at the Ministry of Information. The Colonel had informed Temple that a few selected lecturers were being sent to the States in an effort to render that nation rather more 'Britain conscious.' It was essential that these lecturers should be known to the American public, and the M.O.I. had apparently been to some trouble to discover that the sale

1

of Paul Temple's novels in the States had long since passed six figures. Furthermore, a batch of newspaper cuttings had convinced them that the novelist-detective was also a man of action, who could be relied upon to use his initiative in any unorthodox situation.

So Paul Temple went to America. This time he took his wife with him, and when the lecture agency who made Temple's arrangements discovered that Steve was also an author – of 'The Front Page Men,' which had enjoyed enormous popularity in the States, following the sensational reports of the activities of this gang of criminals in England – then Steve's services were also very much in demand, and she was booked for a long series of lectures to women's organisations of every description. So strange, indeed, were some of them that Steve felt that the association in question should be lecturing her on its peculiar origin.

However, Paul Temple and Steve ultimately arrived at Chicago. They marvelled at its luxury hotels, eyed its stockyards somewhat dubiously, walked the full length of the celebrated waterfront, and finally reached the luxurious portals of Station GSKZ, where Paul Temple was due to be interviewed on the air that evening by Cranmer Guest, whose reputation as radio's ace interviewer conjured a thousand dollars from the pockets of his sponsors every time his programme went on the air.

This was the first time Temple had visited an American broadcasting station, though he had been on the air several times from the stately building that dominates Langham Place. Station GSKZ was a very different proposition however from the somewhat austere atmosphere of Broadcasting House.

It was five minutes to seven o'clock, and Paul Temple and Steve found themselves enveloped in the crowd which was surging through the foyer of the studios; it reminded the novelist of fighting for admission to a Hollywood premiere. There was apparently a theatre on the ground floor level, and a large notice near the door informed the visitors that the 'Laughing Cavalier' programme was to be broadcast from this particular auditorium at seven o'clock. Temple and Steve had some difficulty in avoiding being swept in with the mass of people who were presenting yellow tickets to the page-boy at the door. However, they eventually extricated themselves and headed for a desk in an opposite corner of the foyer which was marked 'Information.'

The blonde in charge could best be described as 'snappy' in the more pleasant sense of the word.

'Laughing Cavalier programme in the auditorium,' she announced, mechanically before Temple could make any inquiry.

Temple smiled.

'I'm sure the Laughing Cavalier is quite a delightful person to meet,' he replied, urbanely, 'but I doubt if we'd have much time for each other at the moment.' The blonde raised her eyebrows almost imperceptibly and favoured him with a noncommittal stare.

'Were you wanting to see someone?' she asked.

'Yes – a Mr. Cranmer Guest,' replied Temple, casually.

'Cranmer Guest? Oh, you can't see him. He's busy with his programme – goes on the air at nine,' she quickly informed him.

'I'm afraid Mr. Guest won't go on the air at nine, unless I happen to be present,' said Temple suavely. The receptionist took a quick glance at her copy of the programme schedule.

'Say – you wouldn't be Paul Temple?'

'I usually manage to keep my appointments,' he smiled.

'Oh, I beg your pardon, Mr. Temple,' she apologised, pushing in a plug on the nearby switchboard. 'I'll tell Mr. Guest right away.'

She spoke into the receiver, and presently announced: 'Mr. Guest will be right down.'

As Temple was turning away she reached for a pale blue envelope that lay in a pigeon-hole at her side.

'Mr. Temple, this message came for you over short-wave from London. It's been sent on from New York.'

Temple scrutinised the envelope, then thrust it into his pocket. He was just moving away when he turned and asked the girl: 'Supposing there's an answer to this – can I send it from here?'

'Sure thing,' she smiled. 'We've got a special short-wave service here for priority stuff; it's working day and night.'

'Whatever can it be, darling?' Steve asked as they sat down on a settee near the information desk.

'I expect it's in code – it'll have to wait till after the broadcast,' he replied, as a thickset man with a very large head, slightly crooked nose and a mobile mouth came towards them.

He exchanged a glance with the receptionist, then addressed Temple.

'Welcome to GSKZ, Mr. Temple.'

Temple rose and shook hands, then introduced Steve.

'This is a pleasure,' said Cranmer Guest with a disarming smile. 'Shall we go up to my office?'

'Would you like me to wait here?' interposed Steve.

Guest waved aside the idea.

'Certainly not, Mrs. Temple. We have a comfortable lounge and restaurant upstairs. Come along with us – and after the broadcast I'll show you round.'

He led the way to the elevator, past the doors of the auditorium, now closed, through which came the very faint strains of a popular dance tune.

The elevator stopped on the fourth floor, and Guest led them down a broad corridor containing numerous signs: Studio 4A, Control, Studio 4B, Artistes' Room, Announcers, News Room, Lounge and Restaurant. They saw Steve settled with a magazine and a cup of coffee, then went into Guest's office, which had his name painted on the door in small black letters.

'This is Miss Wharton, my secretary – Mr. Temple,' announced Guest as they entered the room, and a dark, intelligent girl looked up from her typewriter. 'Now Lesley, here's another rush job. Take down Mr. Temple's answers to my questions and let's have your copies right away. We're on the air in' – he looked at the wall clock – 'less than two hours.'

Without any further ado, Guest began to fire questions at his visitor. They were chiefly concerning Temple's crime experiences. The questions were shrewd and, in an indirect manner, displayed a considerable knowledge of the subject. But Guest was not interested in airing his own knowledge. He let Temple go on talking as long as he wished; then after about half-an-hour's conversation, during which the secretary had busily filled several pages of her notebook, Guest sighed in some relief.

'There, I think that's about all, Mr. Temple. I think this should make just about the best interview I've tackled this year. Glad the network's taking it.' He paused, then added as an afterthought: 'Oh, just one more question. Do you know anything about this person who calls himself The Marquis?'

Temple shook his head.

'Only what I've read in the papers. His – er – activities seem to have come to light since I sailed.'

'H'm,' murmured Guest, 'the police over there don't seem to be making much headway. The fellow just commits one murder after another and, so far as I can make out, gets away with it. You ought to see the headlines in a batch of English papers I received yesterday.' He paused, then added curiously: 'I suppose Scotland Yard haven't sent for you by any chance?'

Temple smiled. 'Not to my knowledge,' he replied, in some amusement.

'Oh well,' shrugged Guest, turning to his secretary. 'That last question's off the record, Lesley.'

As quickly as Miss Wharton typed out the contents of her notebook, Guest and Temple went through them, deleting a sentence here and there, adding an occasional explanatory phrase, sometimes re-writing a whole paragraph. When they had finished, Guest read through the final version with a stopwatch in his hand, and discovered that they would over-run by two minutes. So another question and answer were cut out. The final result was passed back to Miss Wharton to make a final draft.

Guest stood up and stretched himself.

'Twenty-five minutes before we're due on the air. Time for a cup of coffee with Mrs. Temple,' he announced, offering Temple a cigarette.

In the lounge, a loudspeaker, turned right down, was playing dance music which was being broadcast at that moment on a network programme from New York. Just as they had joined Steve, a breathless young man in an open shirt came up to Guest.

'Same layout, Cran?' he asked.

Guest nodded.

'Twelve minutes,' he replied. 'One minute commercial to start and finish, and the introduction for Mr. Temple I gave you this morning.'

The young man smiled at Temple.

'This is Harvey Lane, one of our announcers – Mr. and Mrs. Temple,' Guest introduced them briefly. Lane chatted pleasantly for a minute, then made a hurried departure.

'Never a minute to breathe, poor devils,' commented Guest, stirring his coffee. 'Oh well, we've all had to go through it – station breaks, forenoon plugs, lunchtime commercials – it's all in the game.'

Temple and Steve exchanged a smile.

'How's it going, darling?' she asked.

'I shan't be sorry to see the clock pointing to nine-fifteen,' he admitted, dryly.

'Perhaps Mrs. Temple would like to come in the studio,' suggested Guest.

Steve shook her head. 'I'd much sooner listen in here,' she declared.

At ten minutes to nine, Guest led the way into a small studio, where the main object of furniture was a flat-top desk with two microphones on it. There was a chair in front of each microphone, and on the opposite wall was a large clock with a red second hand slowly moving round the dial. Under the clock stood a large window commanding a view of the control room, complete with its gramophone turntables and banks of meters.

At one minute to nine, after Temple and Guest had settled themselves comfortably in their chairs, Miss Wharton rushed in with the completed scripts.

Guest began glancing through his copy. 'Plenty of time to look through it,' he told Temple, as the announcer came in and took his stand in front of a microphone.

The engineer behind the glass panel held up his hand. Ten seconds to go. Temple had always found these last few seconds before a broadcast completely awe-inspiring. One hardly dared to breathe. It was as if some world-shattering event, like the downfall of an empire, was due to take place at the split second of nine o'clock.

There was the sound of a distant fanfare of trumpets – played on a record in the Control Room – and the engineer dropped his hand. Harvey Lane faced the microphone squarely.

'The Pan-American Fruit Combine brings you the Cranmer Guest programme!' he announced impressively ...

They finished promptly at nine-fourteen, and following a significant jerk of Guest's head, Temple rose and joined him outside the studio.

Steve rose to meet them as they came through the door.

'I'd no idea I had married such an accomplished actor,' she smiled. 'You both sounded extremely professional.'

'Forget it!' said Temple laconically, and Cranmer Guest laughed. 'Care to take a look round while you're here?' he offered, and proceeded to conduct them over the large building, where Steve was particularly impressed by the News Rooms with their tape machines ticking busily and sub-editors frowning beneath gaily coloured eye-shades.

When they stood in the foyer once again amid a crowd queuing up for the 'Southern Skies' programme, billed to take place at ten-fifteen, the Temples shook hands with Guest and bade him good night.

'Where to now?' asked Steve as Temple summoned a taxi.

'A little speakeasy I used to know in Prohibition days,' he told her. 'Rather a cosy little place – they used to call it Maisie's Craze.'

He gave this name to the taxi-driver who shook his head.

'Maisie don't live there any more, brother. They call it the Appenine Club these days.'

'All right,' agreed Temple. 'Take us there.'

But the Appenine Club proved disappointing, at any rate to Temple.

'It isn't the same without Maisie,' he sighed regretfully, as they sat eating an indifferently cooked supper. He turned to the waiter who was uncorking a bottle of wine.

'What's happened to Maisie?' he asked.

The waiter shrugged. 'Last time I heard of her she was in New York, singing at the Three-Fifty.'

'Who is this Maisie, anyway?' asked Steve.

'Oh, just a friend of mine,' replied her husband, with an indifference that would have intrigued any woman.

'Did you know her very well?' persisted Steve.

'Quite well! She was a very human sort of person. We had a lot of fun together in the old days.' Steve noted the distant light in his eyes, and was more curious than ever. But she managed to restrain her curiosity, and after witnessing a very second-rate cabaret act, they returned to their hotel. It was not until he was taking off his coat to put on a dressing-gown that Temple remembered the blue envelope he had thrust in his pocket. He took it out and examined it, then carefully slit open the flap. Inside, there was a piece of blue paper headed 'Station GSKZ. Special Short-Wave Message transmitted from London, England.' The message itself, though short, was in code.

Temple picked up his keys and unlocked his travelling trunk. He pressed one of the studs on the outside and a part of the side of the trunk snapped back. From the half-dozen miscellaneous articles Temple chose a tiny notebook. With the book's help he decoded the message in rather less than two minutes. It ran:

*

'*Request immediate return to assist investigation of the Marquis murders. Cartmell. Home Secretary's Office.*'

Temple was just returning the code book to the trunk when the bedside telephone buzzed.

'This is Jefferson, Programme Supervisor, GSKZ,' said a strange voice when Temple had spoken. 'Mr. Temple, we all liked your little talk tonight. I was dining with J. C. Marriman – he was very much impressed and asked me to invite you to take part in his company's "Grand Parade" programme tomorrow at eight.'

'I'm sorry,' said Temple definitely.

'But look here, Mr. Temple, if it's a question of money, I know J.C. will be quite willing to—'

'No, no,' interposed Temple. 'I'd have been glad to help you, Mr. Jefferson, but it just isn't possible. I have other plans.'

The Programme Supervisor pleaded for some minutes, but Temple remained firm, and finally he rang off. As he replaced the receiver, Steve asked: 'Darling, what are your other plans?'

Temple flung himself into an armchair and lighted a cigarette.

'I'm afraid this is very sudden – upsets our trip. But it just can't be helped.'

'Is it something to do with that message you've just read?' she inquired. He nodded.

'By Timothy, that reminds me, I must send a reply.' He went to retrieve his code book, then hesitated. 'No,' he decided, 'I'll do it in the morning before we start.'

'Start? Where to?'

He blew a cloud of smoke into the air. 'Back to England, Steve,' he announced calmly.

*

It was fortunate that Steve's experience as a reporter had accustomed her to acting swiftly, and she was up before six-thirty the next morning packing and sending telegrams to secretaries and organisers who were expecting them to lecture at their various gatherings.

At ten o'clock Temple left her still busily occupied, and, having translated his message into code, strolled round to the broadcasting station, to find that the blonde at the information desk had been replaced by a red-head who was even smarter on the uptake.

'Oh Mr. Temple, it's a real thrill to meet you in person,' she blithely informed him. 'I heard you on the air last night. Say, I do like your voice – it's so English.'

Temple smiled his acknowledgment, then stated his errand.

'I understand I can send a code message from here on the short-wave to England.'

'That's right,' she agreed. 'But talking of code messages, there's one waiting here for you.'

'I got it last night, thanks,' he replied, politely.

'Oh no you didn't,' she insisted. 'It only came through this morning just after I signed on.'

Without further ado, she handed him another blue envelope. Temple surveyed it in some bewilderment.

'I think I'd better postpone sending my message until I find out what's in this,' he decided at last, and, bidding the receptionist a pleasant good morning, returned to his hotel.

Steve was just putting the finishing touches to their packing when she noticed him puzzling over the flimsy.

'What's the trouble, Paul?'

11

He shook his head. 'I can't make this out,' he admitted. 'The message is in the secret Home Office code: yet it comes from a complete stranger.'

'Does it make sense?'

He passed over the slip of paper, and Steve read:

I'll be expecting you, Mr. Temple – The Marquis.

CHAPTER II

River Patrol

SERGEANT RUPERT JOSIAH CARRINGTON BRIGGS skilfully guided
the narrow police launch through the churning wake of an
overloaded tramp steamer and past the gaunt cranes and
warehouses which were dimly silhouetted against the heavy
night sky. There came the distant rumble of a storm somewhere beyond Greenwich, and a gust of wind rippled across
the water, bringing a scurry of raindrops in its train.

Briggs had the heavy jowl of a typical Yorkshireman which
gave the effect of an almost perpetual frown, particularly
when he was steering the launch with the aid of a single
heavily shielded headlamp.

He shivered and tightened the strap of his sou'wester.

'If this is the Thames,' he declared, in an embittered tone,
'you can have it!'

A broad grin split the Cockney features of his companion,
Sergeant Hanmer, who had been born within the sound of the
river traffic, and had an extensive knowledge of the famous
waterway in all its moods. No aspect of the river which
carried such a strange assortment of cargoes ever seemed

13

to disturb Hanmer. He began to fasten up his oilskins as he observed cheerfully: 'I told you to look out for a bit of real life on the old river!'

An empty crate bumped into the side and vanished in their wake. Briggs cursed softly and changed the course a fraction.

'A hell of a night!' he shuddered, as the shower of rain developed into a sudden torrent.

'Not fit for a dog! Have to slow her down.'

'If you go much slower, we'll get swept away by the tide,' chuckled Hanmer, who seemed to be enjoying himself. They were making about four knots by this time, and the rush of rain had obscured all sounds save the steady beat of the engine and the occasional hoot of a tramp steamer's siren. The darkness seemed to have reached its maximum intensity, and Hanmer prepared his electric lamp ready for any emergency. Together, they steered unblinkingly through the sheets of rain. Once or twice, Briggs sounded his hooter in a tentative fashion. After a few minutes, the rain almost stopped and the sky lightened a little until they could see very faintly the dim outline of the right bank.

Sergeant Briggs shook the raindrops from his sou'wester and ruminated feelingly on the topic that was always in his mind at such moments as these. Had he been wise to turn down that offer of a job from his wife's father? A nice, steady, nine-till-five job, with an office to himself and a chance of a partnership later on. If only it had been something a bit more exciting than dealing in grate polish! Still, there was a lot to be said for regular hours, leisurely meals, and slippers waiting at the fireside. Sergeant Briggs sighed wistfully.

Hanmer suddenly shook himself like a terrier, and pushed his sou'wester on to the back of his head. Then he took a blackened pipe out of his pocket and thrust it unlighted between his teeth.

'How long have you been in the Force?' he asked presently, in a casual tone. It was Hanmer's stock conversational gambit. He didn't really want to know. What he did want was an opportunity to embark upon an account of his own varied career.

'Me?' muttered Briggs, straining his eyes in the direction of the dim outline of a Norwegian freighter. 'Seventeen years.'

'Blimey!' ejaculated the other, in some surprise. 'You've got longer whiskers than I 'ave!'

Briggs nodded solemnly. 'I joined in August, 1925. I was with the L.C.C. before that.'

'Salvage?' queried Hanmer, the twinkle in his eyes going unseen.

'Not ruddy likely! I was a Grade One clerk,' snapped Briggs. Then he heaved a sigh. 'All the same, it was very tedious. I reckon I must have filled in best part of a million forms of one sort or another in the four years I was there.'

Hanmer laughed.

'Talk about tediousness, you want this job reg'lar. Up and down the ole river night after night.'

He sucked at his pipe reflectively.

'Before this I had a nice little beat in Hampstead. Not much doing, but plenty of good grub in one or two kitchens I could mention. I remember once when I—'

He broke off abruptly and leaned over the side of the boat, gazing intently at a grey object which was only just visible. His electric lamp flashed, startling Briggs.

'Swing her round, mate,' said Hanmer, softly. Briggs immediately shut off his engine, and the boat nosed its way silently towards the grey object which Hanmer kept focused in a circle of light from his torch. Retaining a cautious hand on the wheel, Briggs leaned forward.

15

'Good God, it's a woman!' he exclaimed as they came within easy reach.

'Not much more'n a kid, I reckon,' grunted Hanmer, focusing his light on the face and hair. As they came alongside, Hanmer leaned over and managed to bring the girl's head and shoulders almost into the boat. 'Give us a hand,' he gasped, and Briggs left the wheel to take care of itself for a moment.

Within a few seconds, they had laid the dripping figure of the girl along the well of the motor boat. Hanmer pushed back the sodden hair and whistled softly to himself.

'Another of 'em. She's a goner all right. Looks like she's been in the river for hours.'

'What about trying artificial—' Briggs was starting to suggest, but the other cut him short.

'She's been dead hours. I know the signs. Not a bad looking kid,' he decided. 'We ain't pulled out a real good looker since that houseboat murder – she was an actress – not that she looked much when we got her out.'

Briggs was paying no attention, but had stooped and unfastened the blue mackintosh that clung to the girl's figure. His start of surprise distracted Hanmer who was busy extricating a bulky notebook from an inner pocket.

'What is it? What've you got there?'

With clumsy cold fingers, Briggs was unfastening a small square of white cardboard which was pinned to the girl's dress. Hanmer picked up his electric lamp, and together they examined the sodden pasteboard. Two words were carelessly scrawled in Indian ink. 'Good God!' whistled Hanmer. 'The Marquis!' It must be recorded that Sergeant Rupert Josiah Carrington Briggs experienced an extremely unpleasant sensation in the pit of the stomach.

16

CHAPTER III

Crisis at Scotland Yard

Sir Graham Forbes, Chief Commissioner at New Scotland Yard, was a firm believer in method – and an even greater believer in his own method. And his severest critics amongst the younger members of his staff had to admit that the Chief Commissioner's methods, evolved over a period of many years' experience, usually proved successful. They might provide a number of minor irritants; they might even appear to retard the incidence of Justice, but in the end they were invariably effective. Comparative strangers might deride his absorption in minor routine, but Forbes went his way entirely undeterred. His system had stood so many tests, that he had the utmost confidence in its efficiency.

True, he had encountered one or two setbacks recently in the case of The Marquis murders which were being accorded such extravagant publicity by the press. But Forbes was inclined to make allowances for the press-men. After all, they had to give their readers something lively to read over their breakfast tables and on their tedious journeys to and from work.

That his faith in his system was quite undiminished was demonstrated this fine autumn morning by the presence on his desk of seven folders of varying colours.

There was something reassuring about those folders. They contained every scrap of evidence so far retained in connection with The Marquis murders. It was merely a question of sifting facts in the light of new evidence, Forbes told himself as he listened rather vaguely to the argument which was developing amongst his subordinates. Each of them appeared to have his own theories and plans for substantiating them.

At length, Forbes tapped his desk with his paper-knife.

'Gentlemen, when you've quite finished your little brawl, perhaps we can manage to document one or two more facts. Now Bradley, let's hear what you have to say first. I don't think you've given us a complete statement lately.'

Superintendent Bradley, a sandy-haired, dour individual in the late thirties, shrugged his shoulders impatiently. There was no more reliable man in a tight corner, but he was always inclined to take the law into his own hands, and was notoriously incapable of appreciating the law-breaker's outlook on life.

'There seem to have been too many statements made just lately, Sir Graham, if you want my opinion,' he began, bluntly, indicating the folders. 'You've got a packet of 'em there.'

The others smiled. They knew that Bradley's favourite method was to seize his man and hammer the truth out of him.

'What we want is action!' announced Bradley, decisively. 'And by God we want it now, before it's too late!'

'Look here, Bradley,' snapped Chief Inspector Street, a dark, lanky individual with keen eyes and a sensitive mouth. 'It's all very well for you to talk about action, but you don't seem to realise the devilish cunning of this man we're dealing with.'

'What I realise, Street,' retorted Bradley, the colour mounting at the back of his neck, 'what I realise is that seven people have been murdered – one for each of the Chief's pretty folders. And if it goes on at this rate we shall soon exhaust all the colours of the spectrum.'

Street was about to make an angry reply, but the buzz of the telephone cut him short, and with an impatient gesture Sir Graham lifted the receiver.

'Hullo? I told you not to interrupt Dickson unless—' he paused and his expression hardened. The lines on his face deepened as he listened intently to the message. After a moment, he picked up his Eversharp pencil and made one or two notes on a pad at his elbow. Finally, he replaced the receiver and amid an expectant silence slowly opened a drawer and extracted a magenta folder. As he did so, he turned to Bradley with a grim smile.

'You seem to be a thought-reader, Bradley. We've got another murder on our hands, just as you predicted.' He tore the note from his pad and clipped it neatly inside the folder.

'Who is it this time?' It was Street who spoke.

'A young girl. They picked her out of the river last night,' announced Sir Graham, wearily.

Even Bradley seemed taken aback.

'You mean it's The Marquis?'

The Chief Commissioner nodded. 'They found the usual small square of white cardboard pinned to her dress,' he said.

Inspector Ross, a middle-aged sharp-featured individual, who had spoken very little so far, leaned forward in his chair.

'The man's conceited, Sir Graham,' he pronounced, definitely, 'or he wouldn't go in for all this card business. It sounds to me like Con Landon. We haven't heard anything of Con since he was released six months back.'

Forbes shook his head.

He deplored Ross's weakness of associating known criminals with unsolved crimes. Sometimes it worked, but it was very risky and might mean the loss of a considerable amount of time.

For a few seconds there was silence. Street stood at the window looking gloomily at the traffic rushing along the embankment. At last he turned to ask: 'Have they identified the girl?'

'Not yet,' replied Forbes.

Bradley seemed surprised. 'That's damned odd, isn't it?' he demanded.

'Give the boys a chance,' snapped Ross. 'They only picked the girl out of the river last night.'

Bradley strode excitedly over to Forbes' desk.

'Don't you see what I'm driving at, sir?' he said, forcefully.

'Perhaps you'll enlighten us, Bradley,' replied Forbes, in a patient tone.

'But it's as plain as the nose on your face. All the other victims of The Marquis were well-known people, celebrities in fact. They were identified almost immediately. Myron Harwood! Sir Denis Frinton! Carlton Rodgers! Lady Alice Mapleton! Their death was bound to get into the headlines.'

Sir Graham pondered upon this for a few moments.

'There's something in what you say, Bradley,' he agreed, at length. 'Maybe we'll be able to work on this angle.' Bradley was about to enlarge upon his theory when he was interrupted by the arrival of a sergeant who brought the Chief Commissioner a note marked Urgent and Strictly Confidential. Forbes read it carefully, then let it fall on his desk. He passed a weary hand over his forehead.

'Anything wrong, sir?' asked Bradley.

'No,' answered Forbes. 'Just a note from Paul Temple.'

'Paul Temple!' Both Ross and Bradley spoke at once.

'I thought he was in America,' said Street.

The Chief Commissioner's announcement had obviously aroused some interest. 'Perhaps I'd better read you the note,' he suggested, picking up the paper again. 'It may convey more to you than it does to me.'

He read:

Dear Sir Graham,
Steve and I have just returned from the States. Why
not dine with us tomorrow evening. Shall look
forward to seeing you.

Kindest regards,
Paul Temple.

'Sounds innocent though,' sniffed Bradley.

'Just a minute,' said Forbes slowly. 'There's something else here.' After a pause, he read:

'P.S. Is it true what they say about Rita?'

Ross looked across at Street in obvious bewilderment.

'Is it true what they say about Rita?' Bradley repeated.

'Who the devil's Rita?' asked Ross, in puzzled tones.

'Why has Temple come back, anyway?' Street wanted to know. 'D'you think the Home Secretary has cabled him?'

Any further speculations were cut short by the ringing of the telephone. After a brief conversation, consisting mainly on his part of a series of ejaculations, Forbes swung round in his chair and declared: 'They've identified the girl.'

'Good work,' approved Street. 'Who is she, sir?'

'Her name,' said the Chief Commissioner deliberately, 'was Cartwright. *Rita* Cartwright.'

CHAPTER IV

The Girl Who Knew Too Much

WHEN Steve heard Temple direct the taxi-driver to the nearest airport, she could not repress a start of surprise.

'I had no idea we were going to fly back,' she said, as they settled inside the taxi. 'When did you decide that, Paul?'

'As soon as I received that second message,' he replied, calmly. 'A criminal who is sufficiently on the inside to know that the Home Office had cabled me, and furthermore who has a copy of the secret code, is a man who is going to take some catching. So it seems to me that there's no time to be lost.'

At the aerodrome, they were fortunate enough to secure the last two available seats in a plane which was due to start for New York in just under an hour. When they had partaken of a light meal in the aeroplane, Temple settled down to compose a message to the Home Office, then decided to defer sending it as his code book was not easily accessible. Eventually, he telephoned London just after they landed, and was agreeably surprised to learn that if he applied to the commanding officer of a certain military aerodrome, there would be transport facilities supplied for himself and Steve in the next Liberator to be ferried over.

They found themselves in London four days later.

Pryce welcomed them as inscrutably as ever. Temple had telephoned him from the aerodrome. They were busily unpacking one or two essentials when the man-servant remarked: 'I forgot to mention, sir, that there's a young lady who's rung up several times. A most persistent young person by the name of Cartwright.'

Steve and Temple looked at each other in perplexity and shook their heads almost simultaneously.

'I can't think who it would be,' said Temple.

'Oh, she said you wouldn't know her, sir, but apparently she knows you. And she said it was most urgent that you should get into touch with her as soon as you returned. I made a note of the telephone number on the pad.'

When Temple telephoned Euston 6347 half-an-hour later, a charming feminine voice answered him.

'Thank goodness you're back, Mr. Temple. How soon could I see you? It really is most urgent!'

'Where d'you suggest as a rendezvous?' asked Temple.

The girl hesitated for a moment.

'Do you happen to know a public house off Holborn called The Last Man?' she asked. 'They have a quiet little room at the back. If you could meet me there in half-an-hour, it would be on my way to rather an important appointment I must keep at eight o'clock.'

'I know the place quite well,' Temple assured her, for he was pretty well acquainted with every detail of the district. 'I'll be there in half-an-hour from now.'

When Temple arrived, The Last Man was almost empty. Rita Cartwright was sitting alone in the little room at the back of the saloon bar. Temple was rather taken aback at her extreme youth; judging by the voice on the telephone he had expected someone a great deal older. The girl only seemed to be about twenty: though she was by no means becomingly dressed in a dark mackintosh and a worn green beret. Temple noted that she was drinking neat rum.

'Trying to summon up some Dutch courage,' she explained with a wry smile, after she had introduced herself. 'I've a ticklish job this evening – I've an idea I may have taken on more than I can tackle.' As she spoke the girl shrugged her shoulders and smiled disarmingly.

'Well, I'd better begin at the beginning and tell you I'm a private detective of sorts, and my big job at the moment is investigating the murder of Lady Alice Mapleton. I don't mind admitting that this is my first murder case! And it's certainly some case, Mr. Temple,' she added, with a smile.

'Wasn't that one of The Marquis murders?' asked Temple.

The girl nodded. 'The first. As far as I know, the police are still completely in the dark about it, and if I pull this off it'll be a feather in my cap.'

Temple could not repress a slight smile at her youthful enthusiasm.

'You'll pardon my making such a trite observation,' he said, pleasantly, 'but you're extremely young to be tampering with dangerous criminals.'

She took a gulp at her rum.

'Young I may be – I'm twenty-four to be exact – but I seem to have hit upon clues that so far have evaded the police. But I haven't kept to my story. I'd been established in my present job just under a year when Lady Alice Mapleton was murdered.

I had just recovered a diamond bracelet for the Honourable May Bennerton – rather a tricky job which pleased her a lot. Well, she paid my fee, and I'd almost forgotten the case when she arrived at the office one day with a very superior Society person whom she introduced as the Duchess of Mapleton, the mother of Lady Alice Mapleton. The Honourable May introduced us and then discreetly left us together.'

'Very gratifying,' smiled Temple, offering her a cigarette and lighting it for her. 'And then I presume the Duchess placed her cards on the table?'

Rita Cartwright nodded.

'Like all members of ancient families, she was scared stiff of scandal. But she told me everything she knew: beginning with the fact that Lady Alice was a cocaine addict.'

Temple whistled, thoughtfully.

'That would explain quite a number of things,' he murmured.

'It was obvious that the Duchess was devoted to Alice – she was her only child,' continued Rita. 'And she wasn't at all satisfied by the results the police were getting. But she was afraid to help Scotland Yard by telling them everything she knew because of the unpleasant publicity which might be involved. Her idea then was that with all the extra help she could give me, I could possibly track down the murderer without the full story becoming public. She seemed quite positive that the murderer had some connection with the dope business, and on the face of it I was inclined to agree with her.'

'The theory certainly has possibilities,' Temple agreed.

'And I've explored them thoroughly. The Duchess left me a valuable piece of evidence in the shape of Lady Alice's diary. On the last page there was a pencilled note: Limehouse 7068 – ask for Sammy!'

Temple smiled. 'So you got in touch with my old friend, Sammy Wren,' he said. The girl laughed.

'Right first time. I asked him if he could get me some of the dope, and he fell for it. I went along to an address in Bombay Road and collected the stuff. I've been there several times since, and it's put me in touch with quite a number of the gang. However, up till now, they've always been subordinates, referring to the head man in awed whispers. I could never get the merest inkling about him, until this week I decided to force their hand.'

'You appear to be a very daring young woman,' said Temple, admiringly. 'Exactly how did you force their hand?' Rita stubbed out her cigarette.

'I told them I had an order for about five times the usual quantity, but it was essential that I should see the Chief to make certain arrangements for the distribution of it. One of them went into the next room and made a telephone call: when he came back he said I could see the Chief at eight o'clock tonight.'

Temple flicked the ash from his cigarette and looked at the clock. It was ten-past seven.

'And you've conducted all these investigations entirely on your own?' he asked.

'Practically. In the course of making them, I've run across a young fellow named Roger Storey, who was engaged to Lady Alice, and seems to have some vague idea of exacting a terrible revenge for her death. He's one of those innocuous young men with plenty of money and unlimited time on his hands. We've met several times and discussed many theories about the murder. He helped me to follow up some investigations about a man named Sir Felix Reybourn.'

Temple looked up, quickly.

'The Egyptologist? What about him?'

'Nothing really definite, apart from the fact that he was, as far as we can trace, the last person to see The Marquis victims alive.'

'That's very remarkable,' said Temple with a thoughtful frown. 'Are you quite sure about it?'

She shook her head. 'I'm still working on that angle of the case – of course, if Sir Felix turns up to our appointment tonight, then it'll be quite straightforward. All the same, keep it under your hat for the time being.'

Temple pressed the bell and ordered more drinks.

'I really must congratulate you on a smart piece of work,' he said. 'There's one aspect of the business really puzzles me though.'

'What's that?' she asked.

Temple placed her drink in front of her and added soda to his whisky.

'What puzzles me is the reason why you are so anxious to tell me all this?'

The girl smiled.

'The Duchess of Mapleton has several influential friends at the Home Office. Last week, she told me that you were being called in on the case. She was rather worried because she thought you'd be sure to get on to the dope business. So I suggested that I should take you into our confidence and leave the rest to your discretion. I said that according to *Who's Who*, you had been educated at Winchester and Oxford, and that seemed to pacify the old dear.'

Temple laughed.

'I'm sure I couldn't wish for a more intelligent partner,' he declared, sincerely. 'But I really think you should allow me to come with you tonight.' The girl shook her head most emphatically.

'No, no—that would ruin everything. I'm not aiming at a showdown in the Bombay Road. I just want to discover the identity of the leader. After that, it ought to be plain sailing.'

'As a precaution, Miss Cartwright, would you mind telling me the number of the house in Bombay Road?'

'Why, of course, it's 79A. But promise you won't interfere in any way. If I can pull this off myself, it'll be a feather in my cap.'

'It'll be a complete head-dress,' Temple assured her, with a twinkle in his eye. 'But I would like to add a word of warning.'

'Well?' she smiled.

'Don't be too certain about the plain sailing. My own experiences have always lain amongst some very rough seas.'

Rita picked up her handbag and tucked it under her arm.

'I've been lucky so far,' she said, lightly. 'Maybe my luck will hold.'

But there was a look in her pale blue eyes which seemed to doubt her words.

Sir Graham Forbes stirred his coffee and reflected that Paul Temple and Steve had changed very little since the days when they had joined him in the relentless pursuit of the Front Page Men. If anything, Temple was perhaps a trifle more sunburnt and had possibly lost a little in weight.

During dinner they had talked mainly of Paul Temple's visit to the United States, and Forbes had many questions to ask concerning the F.B.I, and other officials whom he knew out there. It was not until he had half-drained his cup of coffee that Forbes suddenly demanded: 'What did you mean exactly by that postscript?'

Temple knocked the ash off his cigar and frowned thoughtfully. At length, he said:

'Out in the States, Sir Graham, I was attached to the "C" branch of the M.O.I.'

'I gathered you were up to something of that sort from what Colonel Randall told me,' nodded Forbes.

'While we were there,' Temple continued, 'the newspapers started spreading their front pages with a story about this fellow called The Marquis. At first, I thought the whole business was grossly exaggerated, but one evening about a week ago I received a special radio message from the Home Secretary's office that rather changed my ideas, and I knew then ...' He hesitated.

'You knew then that, to put it mildly, things were getting pretty serious.'

Paul Temple smiled in some relief as he realised that Forbes knew rather more than he had anticipated. 'I didn't particularly want to leave the States, Sir Graham. It was interesting work out there – always something moving, and I was beginning to show some results. But I could hardly ignore that message.'

Sir Graham placed his cup on the table and leaned forward.

'The Home Secretary had a very good reason for sending for you, Temple,' he declared quietly. 'I realised a month ago that you were the only man for certain aspects of this job. We need your help, Temple, that's the long and short of it. We need your help pretty badly.'

Temple and Steve exchanged an understanding glance.

Temple said: 'I'm very relieved to hear all this from you, Sir Graham. You know I've never had any desire to intervene in any of your cases, and I've no intention of doing so now if—'

'Don't talk nonsense, darling,' interrupted Steve, refilling Sir Graham's cup. 'You know perfectly well that you have every intention of intervening. And you still haven't answered Sir Graham's question about Rita Cartwright.'

'Yes,' said Forbes, 'I want to hear more about that young lady.'

Temple scratched a match and applied it to his cigar.

'I've only a few sketchy sort of facts, Sir Graham, but I gather that Rita Cartwright is a girl who always wanted a career that was "different." So, heaven help her, she became a sort of private inquiry agent. She's had a certain amount of luck, including a commission to inquire into one of The Marquis murders. The next time I see her however, I intend to advise the—'

'There'll be no next time,' put in Forbes gloomily. 'The body of Rita Cartwright was picked out of the Thames last night. A few hours later, it was identified by a young fellow named Roger Storey.'

Temple wrinkled his forehead. 'That name's familiar.'

'Yes, he's Lady Alice Mapleton's fiancé. Rather an interfering young devil, but we let him down lightly as a rule. The poor fellow's had a bad time. They were to have been married in a few months.'

'There's one thing I haven't mentioned about Rita Cartwright,' said Temple, slowly. 'When she left me last night, she was going to keep an appointment with the leader of a dope-running organisation …'

Sir Graham looked up quickly. 'Eh? Where?'

'At 79A Bombay Road. I'm given to understand that she has been going there for several weeks.'

Sir Graham was plainly impressed, and going over to the telephone, dialled a number and gave some rapid instructions.

'I'm afraid your men won't find very much there,' said Temple, as Sir Graham replaced the receiver.

'Oh – why?'

'Isn't it obvious that Rita Cartwright met The Marquis last night? And I have an idea he's much too clever to leave any clues behind.'

'M'm, maybe you're right,' murmured Forbes, biting hard on the stem of his favourite pipe. For a few minutes they smoked in silence, each busy with his thoughts. Steve went into the dining-room to make up the fire. After a while, Forbes said: 'There are certain aspects of this case which remind me of the Carson blackmail affair! And talking of the Carson business, what's happened to Sammy Wren? He was pretty deeply concerned in that set-up.'

'Oh yes,' agreed Temple, 'I remember Sammy Wren.'

'I've been thinking quite a lot about him just lately,' continued Forbes. 'As a matter of fact, I told Bradley to pick him up about a fortnight ago, thought he might be able to give us a line on this case. But he doesn't seem to be around his old spots. Sam's a queer little devil, but he covers a lot of ground. Seems to know everybody and everything. Probably knew Bradley was after him, and thought we'd caught up on him over some job or other.' He paused as he noticed Temple was smiling, and asked, 'Have I said anything funny?'

'I'm sorry,' apologised Temple, 'I was just thinking about The Golden Cage.'

Forbes was obviously mystified. 'The Golden Cage?'

'Yes, it's a public house near the Elephant and Castle. D'you know it, Sir Graham?'

'No, I can't say I do.'

'It's in one of those narrow back streets,' Temple explained. 'You'll find it's frequented by quite an old friend of yours.'

Forbes removed his pipe and slowly smiled. He realised that Paul Temple was referring to the illusive Sammy Wren.

CHAPTER V

No Beer for Sammy Wren

UNLESS you knew the district fairly well, you could easily pass The Golden Cage without noticing that it was a licensed house. True, there was a sort of drab signboard over the front door, but the paint had long since faded and the lettering was quite indistinct. However, this in no way deterred the supporters of this little hostelry, who were emphatic in their insistence that no better beer was to be found south of the river.

Paul Temple agreed with their verdict. He had discovered The Golden Cage years ago when seeking material for his second novel. Someone had told him that it was a popular rendezvous for members of the criminal fraternity. He had discovered that this was an exaggeration, but, by way of compensation, he also discovered that the Extra Special home-brewed beer which was so much in demand actually tasted of hops. Temple had never forgotten the tang of that rich brown beverage.

'So this is where you used to spend your leisure moments, Mr. Temple,' said Steve, jokingly as they settled in a murky

33

corner of the Smoke Room. The room was crowded with that strange mixture of humanity peculiar to the Elephant and Castle neighbourhood. There were only two other women present, but the regulars did not seem to notice Steve, who was wearing, especially for the occasion, an inconspicuous costume and a somewhat shapeless felt hat.

Temple laughed at his wife's remark, lighted a cigarette, and retorted: 'Don't be silly, darling. All my leisure moments were spent with an exotic blonde from Pimlico. Didn't I confess all that before you married me?'

'It must have slipped your memory, darling!'

'In that case, I'd better buy you a drink. What would you like?'

'A dry Martini,' decided Steve, promptly.

'Not here, it isn't done,' he reproved her. 'We'll begin with two pints of their Extra Special.'

'One and a half – in case I don't like it.'

He beckoned to the barmaid, who was standing with her back to Steve, engaged in lively repartee with a group of young men. As she swung into view, he recognised her at once.

'God bless my soul, if it isn't Dolly Fraser!' he exclaimed.

The girl's heavily made-up features showed the merest trace of fear before they resumed their former brazen expression.

'The name's Smith – Betty Smith,' she answered, sullenly.

Temple smiled whimsically.

'Not one of the Shropshire Smiths?' he demanded, with the merest flicker of an eyelid in Steve's direction.

'And what if I am one of the Shropshire Smiths?' challenged the girl, with a toss of her coppery hair.

'Would it, in that case, be too much to ask you to bring us a tankard and a glass of your Extra Special?' demanded Temple, politely.

'Special's off – been finished months ago,' replied the girl, brusquely, pushing back a lock of hair. 'I'll bring you some Old Ale if you like. That's the best we've got.'

'Thank you, that would do nicely,' said Temple, suavely. With an insolent lift of the shoulder, the barmaid vanished. When she was out of earshot, Steve asked: 'Do you know that girl, or was that merely a sample of your sales talk?'

Temple grinned.

'I know her all right. Her name is Fraser – Dolly Fraser. She was one of the shining lights of the Reagan crowd a few years ago. One of the most useful decoys in the game – she's quite an actress in her way.'

He spoke in a carefully modulated tone, but apparently he was overheard by a tall, thin man who could not find a seat, and was leaning against a partition nearby.

'That's quite right, Mr. Temple,' confirmed the stranger. 'Her name is Fraser, and she was with the Reagan mob about two years ago when they pulled off the Charteris kidnapping.'

Temple and Steve swung round. The newcomer suddenly found a high stool and perched himself on it, apparently quite at ease.

'Forgive me if I am intruding, but I couldn't help overhearing your remark, Mr. Temple. My name is Ross – Inspector Ross of the C.I.D. I think we met just before you sailed for America.'

'Why of course, Inspector! I'm afraid I didn't recognise you,' said Temple, pleasantly. 'Have you met my wife?' When the introductions were complete, Temple invited the Inspector to join them in a drink, but he shook his head regretfully.

'No thanks, Mr. Temple. I've had my allowance. I really ought to have been home hours ago. This is an off-duty visit.'

'All the more reason for a little relaxation,' urged Temple, but Ross would not be persuaded to change his mind, and eventually bade them good night. 'I'm keeping an eye on Dolly Fraser,' he assured Temple in an undertone just before he turned to go.

'Is he one of the new people at the Yard?' asked Steve, when the lanky form had disappeared.

'No. He's been there for longer than I care to remember. He used to be attached to the Fingerprint Department till Bradley took over. I don't think they get on very well together. Anyhow, Forbes decided to transfer Ross; gave him a sort of roving commission, and he's turned up trumps several times. He has the reputation of being a pretty shrewd sort of fellow.'

By this time, Dolly Fraser had returned, and was placing their beer on the table. As Temple fumbled for half-a-crown, she seemed about to speak, hesitated, then finally ventured:

'I'm sorry I was rude just now, Mr. Temple. It was that Ross – he's always hanging round here – gets on my nerves. Why can't he leave me alone?'

'Take it easy, Dolly. No harm done,' smiled Temple.

'It was silly of me to say my name's Smith. I've done nothing to be ashamed of,' she added with a touch of defiance.

'Of course you haven't.'

'I knew you'd spotted me the moment you came in,' she continued, rather nervously. 'And what with Ross being there as well – it sort of got under my skin.'

'You thought we'd come to get you for adulterating the Extra Special,' suggested Temple, and Dolly laughed. Then her eyes narrowed slightly, and she could not suppress the curious tone in her voice.

'This is the first time you've been here for ages, Mr. Temple. I suppose you wouldn't be looking for somebody special?'

Temple eyed her, disarmingly.

'Why of course, Dolly. I'm waiting for an old friend of mine. You remember Sammy Wren.'

'Sammy Wren!' she echoed, thoughtfully. 'I haven't set eyes on him for ages.' She paused, then added, significantly: 'Nothin' wrong, I hope?'

'Nothing at all,' he assured her. 'Just a small matter of business. Now, how about having a drink with us?'

'Well, I think a pink gin *would* calm me down a bit,' Dolly admitted, now much more at ease. She returned almost immediately with the drink and Temple's change. Then she fulfilled two more orders and presently drifted over to their table once more.

'So you haven't seen Sammy Wren lately,' said Temple.

'Not for a week or two, maybe more. He used to be in 'ere every day at one time.'

'Is that so? With alcohol taxed as it is, Sammy must be doing pretty well.'

'Maybe,' she replied, indifferently. 'He never tells me his business, and I'm sure I've no wish to know.'

Temple accepted the rebuke. '*You* look fairly prosperous yourself, Dolly,' he said, meaningly.

Some of her former uneasiness returned.

'I'm all right,' she retorted, with a trace of her old defiance. 'The boss 'ere is very good. Quite the gent, if you know what I mean. Only last week, 'e give me a rise. That's the third in eighteen months.'

'That's splendid!'

Dolly relaxed once more. 'Let me get you a gin and tonic, Mrs. Temple,' she suggested, noticing that Steve was not making much impression on the Old Ale. 'We've had a few bottles of real good gin come in this morning.'

As she picked up Steve's glass, Temple suddenly looked up at her and asked: 'Ever heard of this fellow who calls himself The Marquis?'

Dolly almost spilled the beer in the glass, as she dropped it a few inches back on to the table.

'I only know what I read in the papers, and I don't always believe that,' she snapped, glaring down at him. 'Why the 'ell should I know anything about this man? What are you gettin' at?'

'I was only making conversation, Dolly,' apologised Temple, quite meekly.

'Is this a game or what?' she demanded, challengingly. 'You're the second bloke this week who's asked me if I know the ruddy Marquis.'

Temple straightened in his chair.

'Oh? Who was the other fellow?'

She sniffed. 'A young chap called Roger Storey. He's been snooping round here for days asking all sorts of questions. I wouldn't stand for it only, well, he's got a way with 'im, and 'e's lousy with money.' She smiled reminiscently.

'Roger Storey,' repeated Steve. 'That was the young man who identified Rita Cartwright when—'

She stopped speaking as the Smoke Room door swung open vigorously to admit a flashily-dressed little man, who would have looked far more comfortable in a cap and scarf. Sammy Wren came jauntily over to them. From the points of his yellow-brown shoes to the crown of his tilted derby hat, Sammy Wren exuded an air of reckless opulence.

'Hello Mr. Temple, sorry to 'ave kept you waiting.' His was the perkiest brand of Cockney. 'Didn't get your message till late last night.'

Then he caught sight of Dolly and dug her in the ribs.

38

'How's tricks, old gel?' he demanded in a hoarse whisper. She slapped his hand and turned her back on him to take an order from another customer.

Temple introduced Sammy to Steve, who rung her hand fervently.

'Glad to meet your good lady, Mr. Temple. Privilege, I'm sure! I hope you keeps an eye on 'im, Mrs. Temple, and see 'e don't get mixed up in no funny business.' He winked, knowingly.

'Suppose we go into the back parlour,' suggested Temple. 'It's a little more private.'

Sammy consulted an expensive wrist-watch.

'Look 'ere, Mr. Temple, I'm supposed to meet a bloke up West at eight, and it's gone that now. Mebbe you and me could get together tomorrer for a bit of a chat?'

Temple hesitated.

'Where you meeting your friend?' he asked.

'Percy's Snack Bar, just off the Haymarket.'

'Then I'll run you up there in the car,' Temple decided. 'We can talk on the way. Have a drink before we start?'

Sammy shook his head. He was obviously in a hurry, and seemed a little worried. 'Have to be gettin' on, Mr. Temple, if you don't mind,' he decided, and after wishing Dolly good night, they made their way to Temple's car which was parked at the corner of the street. Sammy clambered into the front with Temple, while Steve got into the back seat.

As he settled down at the wheel, Temple reviewed in his mind the salient facts about his companion. Sammy Wren was considered somewhat unique in the underworld, in so far as he did not specialise in any one particular type of crime. Yet he was successful not only in his evasion of the police, but also in the financial reward he derived from his various enterprises. Temple knew that he had tried his hand at blackmail, dope smuggling, passing 'slush,' and forgery. So far, he had only served two short terms of imprisonment, having been able to convince the judge on each occasion that he was a mere accessory to some other unfortunate. There were no flies on Sammy Wren.

As they were heading for the Waterloo Road, Sammy asked: 'What was it you wanted to see me about, Mr. Temple?'

Temple changed gear and passed a large lorry.

'Can't you guess?' he parried.

'Search me,' said Sammy. 'Soon as I got your note, I says to myself: "Allo, something's in the wind, or 'e wouldn't be writin' to a blinkin' tea-leaf like Sammy Wren."'

Temple deftly extracted a cigarette from his case and lighted it with his left hand.

'First of all, Sammy, tell me what happened to Rita Cartwright,' he demanded.

'Cartwright?' repeated Sammy, in genuine bewilderment. 'I don't know anybody o' that name.' Temple gave him a suspicious look out of the corner of his eye.

'I hate to call you a liar, Sammy,' said Temple mildly, 'but I have first-hand information that you made an appointment for her last night at 79A Bombay Road.'

Sammy stiffened in his seat.

'Oh, *that* little so-and-so,' he muttered. 'I didn't know that was her name.'

'Then you do remember?'

Sammy licked his lips.

'Yes,' he admitted, at last, 'I remember.'

'No doubt the boss was very annoyed with you, Sammy, when he found out she was a private detective?'

'So *that's* what he wants to see me about,' breathed Sammy, in some dismay.

'Oh – so you have an appointment with him up West, eh?'

''Ere, what's this, third degree?' demanded Sammy, truculently.

Temple slowed down to avoid a tram.

'You knew, of course, that Rita Cartwright's body was picked out of the Thames last night,' he said in a casual tone.

'No, I didn't – straight, I didn't!' Sammy protested, hoarsely, and indeed it did appear as if the news surprised him. 'I ain't 'ad nothin' to do with that. You know me, Mr. Temple. I draw the line at murder ...'

'All right, Sammy,' said Temple, softly. 'If you don't know anything about Rita Cartwright's death, perhaps you can enlighten us about The Marquis.'

In the faint blue light from the dashboard, Sammy's features were distorted with doubt and fear.

'The Marquis?' he repeated. 'I don't know nothin' about 'im. I don't want to know nothin' about 'im. And if you takes my tip—'

Temple snatched at the wheel as they lurched dangerously towards a bus that was running down from Waterloo Bridge.

'Do be careful!' cried Steve, in considerable alarm.

'This steering seems to be playing tricks,' murmured Temple, gently easing the wheel. 'Ah, that's better ...' The car was now proceeding quite normally across the bridge.

'What were you saying, Sammy?'

'I was saying I don't know a thing about this 'ere Marquis – and that's the truth.'

'The whole truth and nothing but?'

'You know me, Mr. Temple. I wouldn't 'old out on you; not for all the bloomin' gold in America.'

'I'll take your word for it, Sammy,' replied Temple, a trifle puzzled nevertheless.

'Funny you should ask me about The Marquis,' mused Sammy. 'I bumped into a bloke at the Black Swan only a week ago, who asked me the same question. Smart lookin' young feller, took him for a "con" man at first, but I was wrong.'

'He didn't tell you his name?'

'Yes, an' I got it on the tip of me tongue! – Storey! – that's it – Roger Storey.' A new thought seemed to cross Sammy's mind.

'Look here, Mr. Temple, he wouldn't be a rozzer, would he? Because if he is, I'll—'

'Paul!' interposed Steve, urgently. 'Pull over for that lorry.' They were rushing along the embankment at thirty miles an hour, but the lorry was rapidly overhauling them. Temple accelerated a trifle, and they drew away.

'This boss of yours, Sammy,' he said. 'Who is he?'

'I don't know, Mr. Temple – honest, I don't. Never set eyes on 'im before. I just got me orders from a feller named Dukes …'

'Then you don't know that 79A Bombay Road was raided?'

'Raided?' Sammy was patently scared.

'It's all right, Sammy – the police didn't find a thing to incriminate you. All the same, I'm coming along to take a look at this boss of yours. Just in case it's—'

'The Marquis?' queried Sammy, with a gulp. 'But I tell yer it can't be, Mr. Temple. The Marquis has got—' He broke off and clutched Temple's arm. 'Look out, sir, or that three-tonner'll bounce us right into the river!'

Temple tugged at the wheel, but the steering seemed to be completely out of action. As the lorry came level, he snatched at the handbrake, but the front wheels of the overtaking vehicle suddenly swung into the car. To the accompaniment of breaking glass, screaming brakes, and the crash of metal they smashed into the wall of the embankment. Sammy Wren was thrown hard against the windscreen, which immediately collapsed, precipitating him between the embankment wall and the bonnet of the car. The driving wheel saved Temple from a similar fate, though the sudden blow in the chest winded him for some time.

Just before the crash, Steve had flung herself on the floor at the back, and so escaped with a shaking.

'Paul!' she cried. 'Are you all right?'

For a minute he was too breathless to reply. Then he wiped the blood from a cut on his cheek, felt his limbs carefully and shook bits of glass from his clothes.

'I'm O.K., Steve,' he announced, eventually. 'How about you?'

When she had reassured him, he suddenly realised that Sammy had vanished. Leaping out of the car, he quickly discovered the little man. By now, the lorry had backed on to the road again, two policemen had arrived on the scene, and a crowd was gathering, avid for details of the accident.

Someone caught Temple's arm, and swinging round he saw, by the limited light from the headlamps, a breathless young man in dark grey flannels.

'I say, are you all right?' demanded the newcomer.

'Help me to move the car,' urged Temple, indicating the spread-eagled form of Sammy Wren.

'Why yes – yes, of course,' agreed the young man. They were joined by the two constables, who assisted them to extricate the unfortunate Sammy Wren, now unconscious and bleeding from a gash at the back of the head. Neither of the constables had a first-aid outfit, but the young man proved surprisingly efficient in contriving a temporary bandage with the help of a couple of handkerchiefs.

When at last the ambulance arrived, and the inert form of Sammy Wren was carried away, Temple turned to the young man.

'Thanks for helping us out,' he said.

The other smiled, a very pleasant, engaging smile, and pushed a strand of fair wavy hair back from his forehead.

'Not at all, I was only too glad to help. I hope the poor devil will be all right. It must have been a shock for you. Your wife, too.' He switched his infectious smile in Steve's direction.

'If you'll excuse me, sir,' he continued, politely, 'your face seems familiar. Aren't you Paul Temple?'

'Yes.'

The young man smote his right fist into the palm of his left hand.

'What an amazing coincidence! I've been trying to get in touch with you all the evening.'

'Indeed?' said Temple, somewhat surprised.

'It's quite providential we should meet like this,' went on the young man exuberantly, reminding Temple rather of an excited undergraduate. 'If you will permit me to introduce myself ...' He paused to get his breath, then said: 'My name is Storey—Roger Storey.'

CHAPTER VI

Roger Storey Explains

As SOON as Sammy Wren had been safely extricated, Temple's next objective had been to discover the driver of the lorry. But the intervention of Roger Storey had temporarily diverted him, and it was Storey himself who gave him a reminder.

'I say, where the devil is the fellow who drove the lorry? I haven't seen him, have you?' Storey spoke in a public school accent that was as unmistakable as his old Harrovian tie.

Temple's brows contracted.

'No,' he replied. 'And I have a hunch we shan't.'

'But surely the fellow can't run away and leave his lorry. I mean to say it could be traced to his boss and—'

'It's just an idea of mine,' put in Temple, gently, 'that the lorry was stolen. However, we can soon check up on that.' He indicated a police sergeant who was approaching them from the other side of the lorry.

'Nasty smash, sir. Anyone else hurt?'

'Just the one case, sergeant. Pretty hopeless, I'm afraid.'

The sergeant nodded. 'I'll have to make one or two enquiries, sir, if you don't mind,' he continued.

'Yes. I'm rather anxious to make some myself,' said Temple. 'If you'll flash your torch, I'll show you my identity card.'

The sergeant complied, and even before he read the name, was duly impressed by the special card.

'Sorry I didn't recognise you, sir, in this confounded blackout,' the sergeant apologised.

'That's all right. I don't suppose I look exactly present-able with this blood all over my face. Is there a hotel anywhere near?'

'Yes, sir, the Regency. Fifty yards up this turning on the right-hand side. You can't miss it.'

Temple turned to the other two.

'Would you mind taking my wife along to the Regency, Mr. Storey?' he asked. 'She's a little upset by the accident.'

'Why of course,' agreed Storey, taking Steve's arm. 'I know the Regency – we'll be in the front lounge if you should want us, Sergeant. Though I expect Mr. Temple will be able to give you all the details.'

The sergeant grinned knowingly.

'I shan't be long, darling,' Temple told his wife. 'Just one or two small matters to clear up.'

'Don't forget, we'll be in the lounge,' called Roger over his shoulder as they disappeared into the night. 'Now, what you want, Mrs. Temple, is a jolly good double brandy. Pre-war strength, if they've got it. And by gad, I could do with one myself ...'

Temple smiled as the voices slowly faded. Then he turned to the sergeant, who was peering round the car with the help of a torch.

'Now Sergeant,' said Temple, 'what about this lorry driver?'

'That's just the mystery, sir. Neither of my men saw him. First of all, they were busy helping with your friend, and by the time they'd finished the man seems to have vanished. Funny business, if you ask me.'

He directed his torch on the steering column of Temple's car, jerked the wheel from side to side, and finally pulled the steering rod out of the socket. At the base of the rod were the unmistakable scratches made by a heavy file.

'Funny sort of accident, this, Mr. Temple,' murmured the sergeant. 'I don't like the look of it.'

'I'm not exactly delighted myself,' said Temple, dryly. 'But I haven't time to investigate now. If you have any questions to ask, sergeant, perhaps you'll come with me ...' He signalled a passing taxi. 'I have an urgent appointment.' The sergeant entered the taxi and Temple paused to give the address.

'Percy's Snack Bar, just off the Haymarket.'

By the time the sergeant had taken down the routine details concerning the accident, they had arrived at their destination. Percy's Snack Bar seemed to have a similar *decor* to the old-time coffee houses, which had no doubt been the inspiration of its designer.

'I'd be glad if you'd come in with me, sergeant, and see if you recognise anybody,' said Temple.

It was evidently a slack time of the evening for no one was sitting at the small tables, although a few people occupied the high stools at the counter.

There was a shabby middle-aged woman moodily consuming a milk-shake, two coltish girls vying for the attentions of a youth, a very old man was noisily drinking soup, and a slim, well-dressed man in the late thirties looked up at them over the top of the evening paper he was reading.

'D'you know that man?' asked Temple of the sergeant.

'Why of course, sir,' replied the latter in some surprise. 'It's Inspector Street! He's one of the new men at the Yard.'

Street leisurely got down from his stool and joined them at the door.

'What's the trouble, Sergeant?' he asked.

'Blessed if I know, sir. Better ask Mr. Temple, here.'

'Oh – so you're Paul Temple,' said Street, eyeing him shrewdly. 'I'm Street – came to the Yard while you were in America.' He spoke in a guarded whisper.

'I can only conclude we're here on the same errand, Inspector,' said Temple quietly. 'How did you get your information?'

'We managed to tap a 'phone call to Sammy Wren.'

'H'm.' Temple looked round the room once more, noting that the clock behind the counter pointed to eight-thirty.

'Any luck yet?' he asked.

Street shook his head. 'Sammy must have got wind of us. He hasn't put in an appearance.'

Temple told him about the accident.

'Then it looks as if this rendezvous is a washout,' decided Street, folding his paper.

'You haven't seen anyone you recognise?' queried Temple.

'Not a soul, except ...' he hesitated. 'I did know one old josser – it seems he often comes in here for a snack. He left about ten minutes ago. Quite well-known in his own line, though I can't say I know much about that sort of thing.'

'And what is his line?' asked Temple.

'He's an Egyptologist named Reybourn, Sir Felix Reybourn.'

When Temple came into the bright lights of the Regency lounge twenty minutes later, Roger Storey at once noticed the cut on his cheek, and insisted on fixing on it a scrap of adhesive plaster, which he extracted from his wallet. As Steve sipped her brandy and ginger ale, she reflected thankfully that her husband's cut cheek was the only outward sign of the accident as far as they were concerned.

When the glasses were half-empty and the flow of small-talk seemed to be slackening, Temple turned to Roger Storey.

'I should be very interested to hear why you've been looking for me this evening,' he murmured.

Storey took a gulp at his brandy.

'Well, I'm dashed if I know quite where to begin,' he confessed.

Temple gave him a searching glance.

'Supposing you take your time,' he suggested, 'and begin at the beginning.'

Storey frowned thoughtfully as if deciding how to approach his subject. Finally, he turned to Steve.

'I think you knew Alice Mapleton, Mrs. Temple.'

Steve thought for a moment, then nodded. 'Yes, the name comes back to me. We were at school together, but she was junior to me, and I never saw very much of her. And now I think of it, we met again at a party about two years ago. She was a willowy brunette – quite attractive.'

'And Lady Alice Mapleton was, of course, the first girl to be murdered by The Marquis,' put in Temple.

Storey nodded, hesitated for a moment, then said: 'Yes, her body was found on the bank of a stream about four miles from Richmond. She had been strangled.'

Steve shuddered.

'I understand Lady Alice was a friend of yours,' said Temple, quietly. The young man pushed the rather becoming lock of wavy hair from his forehead.

'We were engaged,' he replied simply, making a patent effort to conceal his emotion by lighting a cigarette. After a moment, he inhaled a large quantity of smoke, then slowly expelled it.

49

'That was just over four months ago,' he informed them. 'Four months. It seems like four years whenever I think about it.' He took out a handkerchief and blew his nose vigorously.

There was silence for some seconds, then Temple asked: 'Was your fiancée worried at all?'

Storey shrugged impatiently. 'Haven't you read those awful reports of the inquest? God! It was on every front page!' He seemed to recoil at the recollection.

'We've only just returned from America,' Steve reminded him, gently. He apologised, and continued: 'Yes, Alice was worried. There's no doubt about that. She was terribly worried. Though I admit that she was always a moody sort of girl, and we frequently had the most awful rows. Being engaged isn't all honey, I can tell you.'

Steve smiled at the boyish confession.

'Yes, we had our quarrels,' he continued, 'but we never stopped being in love with each other for a single minute. The night before it happened, we had one of our worst stack-ups. I can't even remember what it was about, but poor Alice had been irritable and difficult to get on with that day. I realise now why she was like that.'

'Please go on,' said Temple.

Roger Storey stubbed out his cigarette with long, nervous fingers.

'It was blackmail!' he muttered in a tense voice.

Steve looked horrified and checked an exclamation.

'You mean The Marquis?' suggested Temple.

'Yes.'

Storey's eyes assumed a distant expression, and his lips narrowed into a thin line. With jerky movements he lighted another cigarette, then continued:

'He's a cunning sort of devil you know, Temple. He puts

50

the pressure on his victims until they can stand it no longer, and then …' his mouth twitched nervously as he seemed to visualise the consequences.

Temple suddenly said: 'Sir Graham Forbes tells me that you identified the body of Rita Cartwright. Is that true?'

'Quite correct,' Roger admitted. 'That takes me a step further in my story. After Alice was murdered, I was so desperately worried, and I suppose almost out of my mind with anxiety, I felt that if I didn't do something definite I'd go mad. So I started making investigations of my own in an amateurish sort of way. It wasn't that I hadn't any faith in the police or Scotland Yard; I just had to do something about it myself.'

'I understand,' murmured Temple, nodding sympathetically, and beckoning a waiter to refill their glasses.

'After I'd made one or two frightful blunders, Alice's mother seemed to get a bit rattled. She told me that she had engaged a private detective named Rita Cartwright, and suggested that I should get in touch with her before making any more moves which might attract unpleasant publicity.' Storey paused, then asked: 'Did you happen to know Rita Cartwright?'

'I met her once,' said Temple, non-committally. 'She struck me as being a very sensible young person.'

Storey nodded.

'Rita was no fool,' he agreed, a note of bitterness creeping into his voice, 'but she wasn't clever enough for The Marquis!'

'Mr. Storey, why do you think Rita Cartwright was murdered?' asked Steve.

Roger straightened himself abruptly, then leaned forward and spoke in a confidential undertone.

'I think I can tell you why, Mrs. Temple. It was because she found out something about a man called Sir Felix Reybourn.'

'You mean the Egyptologist?' asked Temple.

'That's the man.'

'And what did she discover?' asked Steve.

Roger hesitated and nervously fingered his tie.

'Mr. Temple, before I answer your wife's question, will you tell me if I strike you as being a frightened sort of person?'

Temple smiled.

'I don't think so, Storey. Nervous, perhaps. But I'd say it takes quite a lot to scare you.'

The young man moistened his lips, and spoke in almost a whisper.

'Well, I am frightened! Hellishly frightened! And I may as well admit it now before I go any further.' There was a long pause.

'During the past six months,' proceeded Storey, eventually, 'there have been four attempts on my life. Fortunately for me they've proved unsuccessful but now you see why I was so anxious to get in touch with you. I wanted to tell you everything I know, everything Rita Cartwright knew, about The Marquis.'

'Then,' said Temple softly, 'begin by telling us *who is* The Marquis?'

With a wistful half-smile, Roger shook his head. He seemed to have aged perceptibly in the past half-hour.

'If I was quite certain of that, Mr. Temple, I wouldn't be sitting here.'

'But you suspect Sir Felix Reybourn?'

Roger took refuge in an expressive shrug.

'I don't see whom else I can suspect – in the face of all the facts.'

'Suppose you tell us the facts?'

'Take Alice's case first, then: two days before she was murdered, she paid Sir Felix a visit. I don't know why; I've never been able to find out. Twenty-four hours before the police discovered the body of Carlton Rodgers on the beach at Newhaven, he had dined with Sir Felix at his house in St. John's Wood. And the last person to see Myron Harwood alive was Sir Felix Reybourn!'

He paused to note the impression his statement had made.

'You're quite sure of these facts?' said Temple.

'Absolutely certain.'

Steve imagined for a second that she caught a strange, wild gleam in Storey's pale blue eyes. 'Poor boy,' she thought: 'This business is sending him distracted.'

'Did you discover all these facts yourself?' asked Temple.

Roger shook his head.

'I helped to check up on one or two items. But the real work was done by Rita Cartwright.' He hesitated, then: 'And if you want my opinion, Mr. Temple, that's the reason why she was murdered!'

On their return to the flat, Temple and Steve were met by Pryce, who informed them that Sir Graham Forbes and Superintendent Bradley were waiting in the library.

'Are you all right, madam?' asked Pryce, anxiously. 'I heard Sir Graham say something about an accident.'

'Quite sound in wind and limb, Pryce,' his master breezily assured him. 'Bring in some coffee as soon as you can.'

Nevertheless, as soon as Pryce had gone into the kitchen, Temple turned to his wife.

'Sure you wouldn't like to go straight to bed?' he asked. 'You must feel quite worn out.'

'Not a bit of it,' she insisted. 'Remember I was used to working nights in my newspaper days.'

'That sounds rather paradoxical,' he murmured. 'Still, what else could one expect from an ex-reporter?'

She squeezed his arm affectionately, and they went into the library, where Sir Graham and his assistant had made themselves comfortable. As the door opened, Forbes was draining his glass. He turned.

'Ah, so there you both are – at last,' he greeted them.

'It isn't often we have the pleasure of two visits from you, Sir Graham, in such a short time,' smiled Steve, who appeared as fresh and unperturbed as when they had met earlier.

'It can't be much of a pleasure, my dear,' drawled Forbes. 'Not at this time of night.' He turned to introduce Superintendent Bradley, who seemed eager to get to business.

'They 'phoned through to the Yard about the accident, Mr. Temple, and we thought there might have been—'

'Yes,' Temple interrupted. 'But I don't think "accident" is quite the right word, Bradley.'

'H'm, that was my impression,' grunted Forbes. 'You know, you'll have to be careful, Temple. You've started stirring up things pretty actively, and this fellow's dangerous. We never know where he is or what he'll be up to next.'

'What about Bombay Road? Any further developments?' asked Temple.

'No. I'm having the place watched, of course, but you were right when you said it would be too late. The birds had flown, and they haven't left a trace that amounts to anything. I had five men search the place from cellar to attic – they even ripped up the floorboards.'

'I sincerely trust they have replaced them,' said Temple, with a grim smile.

Bradley offered Temple a cigarette.

'I was sorry to hear about Sammy Wren,' he began. 'He was a queer little devil, but I had quite a sneaking regard for him. Out of the ordinary run of crooks, was Sammy.'

'Did he tell you anything, Temple?' asked Forbes.

Temple shook his head. 'Nothing about The Marquis. But, oddly enough, he told me something about a man called Roger Storey. Since then, I've met Storey himself.'

'Oh, we know all about him,' said Sir Graham, in rather a deprecating tone. 'A decent young fellow who's making himself a general nuisance.'

'I can well imagine that,' smiled Temple.

Bradley thoughtfully stroked the bristly hair at the back of his head. 'Lady Alice Mapleton was his fiancée, you know, so we're making some allowances when he gets under our feet.'

'That's very generous of you.'

Temple paced restlessly across the room, picked up a book, replaced it, then returned to confront Forbes.

'Sir Graham,' he burst forth, suddenly, 'do you think we are up against not only The Marquis, but a definite criminal organisation?'

Sir Graham pondered on this for a while.

'Yes,' he decided at length. 'And if you want my opinion, Temple, it's an organisation which is held together by one element alone – blackmail!'

Steve looked up, inquiringly.

'You mean every member of The Marquis' organisation is being blackmailed?' she asked, recalling a similar case in her newspaper days. And a very difficult case it had been while the blackmailer had remained at large. For his victims would tell any lie or employ any subterfuge in his favour to avoid their own guilty secrets coming to light.

'That's just what I do mean, Steve,' Sir Graham was saying. 'In other words, find The Marquis, and your organisation collapses like a pack of cards!'

Temple nodded. 'I've an idea you're right, Sir Graham. By the way, I saw Inspector Street about an hour ago, at Percy's Snack Bar.'

'Yes – yes – he's telephoned me since then,' said Forbes. 'Nothing doing there apparently, Sammy Wren's accident upset that angle. Street didn't recognise anyone there.'

'That's not quite accurate,' said Temple. 'He did recognise one elderly gentleman, Sir Felix Reybourn.'

'The Egyptologist?' queried Bradley, promptly.

Temple nodded.

'I've heard of Sir Felix,' said Forbes, knitting his brows. 'Lives in St. John's Wood – writes books about mummies and so forth. I don't quite see what he has to do with—'

'Just a moment,' said Temple. 'Please understand that I'm only repeating what I've been told, but I'm given to understand that two days before Lady Alice Mapleton was murdered, she paid Sir Felix a visit. Also, that twenty-four hours before the police discovered the body of Carlton Rodgers, he had dined with Sir Felix. And finally that the last person to see Myron Harwood alive, as far as is known, was Sir Felix Reybourn.'

'Yes, that point came out at the Harwood inquest,' put in Bradley, swiftly.

'Good God! This is staggering,' said Forbes, rising to his feet.

'They are facts which can be checked, I should imagine, Sir Graham,' said Temple, equably.

Sir Graham thumped his fist on the padded arm of the chair. 'By heaven, they will be checked too,' he ejaculated, with some force. 'Bradley, you might look into it as soon as we get back to the office.'

Bradley nodded respectfully.

'We haven't told Mr. Temple the real reason for our visit tonight,' he reminded Forbes.

'Jove, I'd almost forgotten,' Sir Graham admitted, so distracted had he been by recent developments. He fumbled in his pocket and produced a grimy envelope.

'When I got home tonight, I found this on the door mat.' He passed over the letter. 'It's from a man called Roddy Carson. Do you know him?'

Temple stirred his coffee.

'Roddy Carson,' he repeated, thoughtfully. 'Yes, I think so. A tough, illiterate bounder. Served a term for dope smuggling about ten years ago.'

'That's the man. Read his letter.'

Temple unfolded the shabby scrap of paper, and with some difficulty deciphered the pencilled message.

Dear Sir Graham,
If I can trust you, meet me at Forard Glen tonight at
12.30. I shall be waiting near the clump of six trees
about a mile from the road. There is something
about The Marquis I got to get off my chest.

Roddy Carson.

Temple carefully refolded the note and replaced it in the envelope.

'Have you tested this for fingerprints, Bradley?'

The Superintendent nodded. 'It's Roddy Carson all right,' he declared, confidently.

'Where is Forard Glen?' asked Steve, who had heard the name, but could not quite place it.

'About six miles the far side of Hampstead Heath.'

'Ross should be there by now,' said Bradley.

'Ross?' repeated Temple, curiously.

'I contacted the Yard straight away,' pursued Forbes. 'Ross and two of the Flying Squad units are on the job. I thought we'd join them at the zero hour, Temple.'

Paul Temple nodded his agreement.

'But we saw Inspector Ross at The Golden Cage,' put in Steve.

This puzzled Bradley. 'Why, Ross lives out Wimbledon way,' he informed them. 'What the devil would he be doing at the Elephant and Castle?'

'That was over two hours ago,' said Temple. 'Quite a lot can happen in two hours.'

'M'm … all the same, I told the boys to pick him up at his home. He said he'd be on call if wanted. I hope they haven't missed him.'

Temple poured himself some more coffee.

'Yes,' he said, quietly, 'I hope so too.'

CHAPTER VII

Death Stalks Forard Glen

RODDY CARSON had always specialised in dope. He knew every contact man in the business, and what was even more important, he knew his own limitations. In co-operation with a certain wizened little man named Sonny Maskell, Roddy Carson had developed a considerable clientele for those familiar small white packets which commanded such exorbitant prices, and returned such a pleasing profit to the vendor. Lately, however, there had been some falling off in this steady income, and Roddy had not been long in discovering the reason. It appeared that he was facing considerable opposition on a fairly large scale, and the organiser of the new concern had apparently enlisted quite a number of the well-informed middlemen who were always ready to place their services at the disposal of the highest bidder. Along with several other of the 'dope' boys, Roddy Carson and his confederate were also being frozen out of the market by various little devices which would have horrified the most unscrupulous dictator, and called for immediate reprisals.

For some days, Roddy had been watching 79A Bombay Road, and on the night Rita Cartwright was murdered he called on Sonny Maskell at the latter's 'one-room flat' somewhere in the precincts of Soho. Resisting the inviting glances of two elaborately perfumed ladies on the stairs, Roddy thrust open the door of Maskell's room.

'I've got the swine at last, Sonny,' he announced, flinging his huge bulk on the bed.

Sonny blinked at him with watery eyes, and pushed over a bottle and glass.

'What do you mean?' he demanded.

'That – swine at Bombay Road,' exploded Roddy. 'I got something on him tonight that'll put a stop to his little games.'

'Go on?' said Mr. Maskell with some display of interest. 'Who is this guy?'

'I seen him go in there once or twice, but I thought he was a customer. Posh lookin' cove with a mackintosh and a soft felt hat pulled down over his eyes. Never took much notice of him before, but I'd know 'im again now. You betcha life.'

'Well, what happened?' Mr. Maskell was growing slowly impatient.

'Plenty! I was 'angin' round the back like I been doin' lately, when suddenly the side door opens. I steps back into the shadows – and out comes this feller carryin' a girl. And if she wasn't a stiff, my name ain't Roddy Carson!'

Mr. Maskell was duly impressed. 'Blimey!' he exclaimed. 'Murder, eh?'

'You said it! I 'ad to dodge up the passage when I 'eard 'im coming back, and just as I passed the side door, it opened and somebody showed a light. I ran like 'ell and just managed to jump on a 'bus at the bottom of the road.'

'Think they recognised you?' asked Sonny.

Roddy shook his head.

'Dunno. Not that it makes much difference.' He balanced his feet on the bedrail and locked his hands behind his head.

'D'yer know what I think, Sonny?' he asked.

'I'll buy it.'

'I think this feller's something to do with The Marquis murders. That's why the police can't find 'im. 'E ain't one of the reg'lars – or I'd know 'im and you'd know 'im.'

Sonny nodded thoughtfully as he absorbed this. 'Think you could spot 'im again?' he asked.

'I'd know that bloke anywhere. It was bright moonlight tonight, and I got a good look at 'is dial.'

'Well, if it should be this 'ere Marquis, you'd be on to a nice reward if you split,' said Sonny.

'You mean that Scotland Yard broadcast last week?'

'That's it – five hundred smackers—'

'And kill two birds with one stone, eh?' murmured Roddy. 'I reckon it's worth tryin'.'

As the police car swept past Jack Straw's, Temple broke a ten minutes' silence to ask Forbes: 'About these cards The Marquis leaves on the body, have you had the writing examined?'

Forbes nodded.

'Yes, but it isn't much help, as we have nothing to compare it with so far. Obviously, we can't rake through specimens of the handwriting of everybody in London. The fellow uses purple sort of ink, but we can't trace it. You see it's quite ordinary stuff that might be bought anywhere.'

'What about fingerprints?'

'No good. The man wears gloves, of course. He never seems to leave anything remotely resembling a clue. No doubt about it, The Marquis has a well-trained criminal mind, either from instinct or experience, and so far the luck's been all on his side. But we'll have to do something pretty soon. The papers are screaming about these mysterious murders, and the Home Office is getting pretty restive as usual.'

'Everything in good time, Sir Graham,' smiled Temple, soothingly. 'What do you think about it, Bradley?'

The sandy-haired superintendent grunted non-committally, but did not venture an opinion. Temple had a suspicion that Bradley was after the kudos of capturing The Marquis, and the promotion it was bound to bring for any member of the Yard staff. Judging by one or two occasional remarks, it seemed that Bradley cherished the idea that Sir Graham was a little too old for his job. That it needed a younger man to hold the reins in these nerve-racking times. But Temple kept his own counsel.

When the car drew on to the grass verge at the roadside and snapped out all its fights, Bradley was the first to get out. In a few moments, a torch flashed fifty yards away to the right, and presently Inspector Ross joined them.

'How long have you been here?' asked Bradley at once.

'I should say about three-quarters of an hour,' said Ross, turning to Sir Graham to explain: 'We've formed a patrol circle, sir. Smith, Warrender, Hale, Dickson and myself with two of the local men.'

'Seen anyone?' asked Forbes, turning up his coat collar.

'Not a soul, sir.' Ross suddenly recognised Temple with a slight start of surprise.

'Hello, Mr. Temple. I didn't see you.'

'No rest for the wicked, eh Ross?'

'That's about it, sir,' replied Ross in a non-committal tone.

The wind whistled through the trees and heavy black clouds rolled up from the west as they walked over to the clump of six straggling fir trees. There was no sign of life.

'Which way d'you think he'll come?' Bradley asked Ross.

'Difficult to say. But he'll be tailed all right. One of the boys is bound to hear him.' Bradley sniffed as if he were inclined to doubt that statement. A torch shone suddenly some distance to their left, and they all halted immediately.

'Who's there?' called Ross sharply. There was no reply. Temple noticed Bradley gently ease his revolver in its holster.

'Is that you, Warrender?' called Ross again.

A figure of a woman suddenly loomed before them.

'It's only me,' said Steve.

Temple bit his lip to conceal his annoyance.

'Steve, you are the limit. I particularly asked you to wait in the car,' he protested.

'But you forgot your torch, I thought I'd better bring it,' she replied, offering him the article in question. The laughter that followed helped to ease the eerie atmosphere. Once more, they moved towards the trees. As they were almost beneath them Bradley suddenly stopped.

'Did you hear that?' he asked.

There was a long, tense pause.

'I'm damned if I can hear anything,' said Forbes petulantly, after they had waited for over a minute.

'You will, Sir Graham,' said Temple, who had heard the sound which had arrested Bradley. 'Quiet now …'

Again they listened, and after a few moments there came a low, soft moan, the last cry of a man who has suffered torture and can endure no more. They heard it again almost at once.

'It's somewhere under these trees, Ross,' whispered Bradley, urgently.

'But damn it, I've just patrolled them half-a-dozen times without seeing a soul.'

'I take it you kept your torch on the ground like a patriotic citizen,' said Temple. Bradley was the first to see the implication of his suggestion.

'My God! He can't be hanging—'

'Listen!' said Temple. Once again they heard the low, soft moan. It seemed to emanate from thin air.

They began a thorough search, and it was not long before they discovered what they sought. The ghastly figure swung, head downwards, suspended by the ankles from a branch fifteen feet above their heads.

'I'll get some brandy from the car,' said Forbes, as one of the Yard men found the other end of the rope and gently lowered the body. Temple examined it quickly.

'I'm afraid it's too late, Sir Graham,' he announced.

'Poor devil,' murmured Forbes.

'Do you recognise him, sir?' asked Ross.

'Yes, this is Roddy Carson all right,' Forbes decided.

Ross went quickly through the dead man's pockets. He unearthed a small revolver and a wallet containing seventeen pounds. The only other thing the wallet contained was a small, empty envelope.

'Looks as if he has jotted something down on this,' muttered Forbes, flashing his torch on it. 'Yes, it's a name and address. Good God – Temple, look here—'

Temple took the envelope and read:

'Sir Felix Reybourn, 492 Maupassant Avenue, St. John's Wood.'

The novelist could not repress a chuckle.

'What the devil's the joke?' snapped Forbes, irritably.

'I was just thinking,' murmured Temple, 'Fancy Roddy Carson being able to spell Maupassant.'

CHAPTER VIII

Sir Felix Entertains

TEMPLE spent most of the following morning delving into the files of the *Egyptologists' Journal* from the past five years. This monthly publication, published from an obscure address near the British Museum, presented a most forbidding appearance to any layman not interested in its particular subject, with its severe buff colour, endless pages of small print and very dull pictures rather indifferently reproduced.

Somewhat to his surprise, Temple found the two articles by Sir Felix Reybourn contained an occasional flash of whimsical humour to relieve their rather erudite discourse. Both concerned a series of excavations undertaken by Sir Felix, which, as far as Temple could see, had proved singularly unproductive save for a few ancient weapons in very poor condition, and a vessel containing a strange liquid which had not been analysed. Sir Felix dilated at some length upon the medicines of ancient Egypt and the cures they were reputed to have effected, and thus he cleverly concealed the paucity of the actual results of his expedition. As a writer himself, Temple admired the ingenious manner in which Sir Felix had contrived this little deception.

By way of an afterthought, he went into another room at the British Museum and looked up Sir Felix in *Who's Who*, but he found the details given were rather scanty, and obviously supplied by the gentleman in question, who had studiously refrained from answering several items on the questionnaire sent him by the publishers. Sir Felix was described as 'Egyptologist and Zoologist'; it appeared he was unmarried, the son of an obscure Cornish baronet, educated at Clifton and London University, where he had gained a B.Sc. with honours. He was the author of a couple of books and several pamphlets on his favourite subjects, though Temple had to admit that he had heard of none of the publications in question, and had a strong suspicion that they were long since out of print.

The address of Sir Felix was given as 492 Maupassant Avenue, St. John's Wood, and as this happened to be the 1935 edition of *Who's Who*, he had obviously been settled there for some considerable time.

Temple stood for a few moments on the steps of the British Museum, and as the sun was shining invitingly, he decided to walk down to Scotland Yard, where he had arranged to meet Sir Graham Forbes at eleven-thirty.

As he walked, Temple turned over the question of Sir Felix Reybourn in his mind, examining it from every possible angle. Why should an elderly man, with apparently an absorbing interest in civilisations of long ago, become in any way involved with modern gangster-dom? What could he hope to gain? Money? Apparently, Sir Felix had managed to obtain finance for several Egyptian expeditions. Was it a case of Jekyll and Hyde again, with the Egyptologist activities as a cloak for diabolical criminal exploits? Or was Sir Felix himself a victim of The Marquis, who was unscrupulously diverting attention from himself by throwing suspicion upon one of his minions? Yet what crime could Sir Felix have committed to bring him within The Marquis' relentless clutches?

Temple strode down Charing Cross Road immersed in thought, bumping into song pluggers, variety artistes, typists carrying tea trays, and milliners' assistants with parcels, and leaving a train of muttered imprecations behind him.

At Scotland Yard he found Forbes in his office, moodily adding fresh details to the evidence in his files, and gloomily reflecting that the aforesaid details amounted to practically nothing at all.

'Pretty folders you have there, Sir Graham,' commented Temple with a smile as he accepted a cigarette. 'They must cheer you up considerably in times like this.'

'Humph!' grunted Sir Graham, pushing four of the folders out of sight. 'Well, what have *you* got to suggest?'

Temple merely took a long draw at his cigarette and strolled over to the window.

'Have you heard of a man named Dukes?' he asked.

'Dukes? There's a little dope peddler named Lannie Dukes.'

Temple nodded thoughtfully.

'That sounds like the man. Think you can find him?'

'Why?'

'He was at 79A Bombay Road. Sammy Wren said he was taking his orders from him.'

'Do you think Wren was telling the truth?'

Temple smiled. 'I think I knew enough about Sammy to ensure that he always told me the truth.'

'All right, I'll put Ross on to Lannie Dukes as soon as he comes in. And now what are you going to do?'

Temple flicked the ash from his cigarette.

'I'm going out to tea on my own invitation,' he announced.

'What the devil—' began Forbes, irritably.

'Steady, Sir Graham. I haven't told you the name of my host yet.'

'I don't see what it has to do with this infernal murder,' snapped Forbes.

'That remains to be proved. You see, I'm proposing to pay a call upon the eminent Egyptologist, Sir Felix Reybourn.'

That afternoon saw Temple and Steve striding energetically past Lord's cricket ground until they arrived at the sweeping curve of Maupassant Avenue, with its pleasant lime trees and dignified Georgian mansions standing well back from the roadway.

Since Number 492 was obviously at least half-a-mile from where they entered the avenue, they strolled on, discussing the mystery of The Marquis in all its latest aspects. Steve suddenly stopped.

'We must have passed it, darling. There's 489 over there, and the numbers run that way—'

'This must be it,' said Temple a minute later, indicating a grey stone building which appeared to be numberless.

'It's between 490 and 494, so by *reductio ad absurdum* ...' Temple was saying, when Steve grabbed his arm.

'Paul, I'm getting scared. What on earth will you say to Sir Felix? Don't you think it would have been better if you had written or telephoned first?'

'And you an ex-reporter!' he chaffed her, lightly. 'Didn't you ever learn anything about the value of the surprise element? Why, that scoop of yours when you interviewed Bernard Shaw would never have come off if you'd written for permission. You just happened to catch him in an idle moment when his thoughts were running on women's suffrage!'

'Darling, this is no joke!' she protested. 'What are you going to say to Sir Felix?'

He turned and faced her as they stood beneath a large yew tree in the drive.

'Well, it's like this. I'm writing a novel – one of those formidable affairs with an Egyptian background—'

'Paul, you never told me!'

He laughed. 'You see, even you believe the story. So now you see why it is absolutely essential that I should check up on certain of my facts.'

'You mean that's why you propose to consult a noted Egyptologist? Well, I suppose it's an excuse – as long as it isn't examined too closely.'

'What d'you mean?'

'He might ask you to tell him the plot of your novel. He might even point out that there's an awful lot of information that can be looked up at the British Museum.'

'I invariably get lost at the British Museum,' he retorted.

'Then there's a good library at Scotland Yard.'

'Or yet again,' interrupted Temple, 'I could take the next plane to Egypt!'

Steve laughed. After a moment, they negotiated a bend in the drive and came to the house.

'You seem a trifle nervous, darling,' he murmured, lightly. 'Think of all the formidable people you interviewed in your newspaper days.'

'That,' replied Steve grimly, 'is precisely what I am thinking.'

Temple laughed as they climbed the steps to the old-fashioned portico, and gave a hearty tug at the ancient bell-knob. Away down a distant corridor, the bell clanged discordantly, but there was no immediate response.

'This is an even bigger house than it looks, I should imagine,' decided Steve, thoughtfully.

'It's obviously quite a strenuous walk from the servants' quarters,' agreed Temple. But at last they heard shuffling footsteps and the sound of an old-fashioned chain being unfastened behind the door. Then a key turned ponderously and a bolt scraped into position. The door opened about a couple of feet, and the pleasant red face of a woman of about sixty-five confronted them. She was a dumpy, likeable little person with a cheerful voice.

'Good afternoon,' she greeted them, opening the door a shade wider, as if to emphasise her welcome. Her deep blue eyes twinkled benevolently, and she looked for all the world like an advertisement for a well-known brand of tea.

Returning her greeting in his most charming manner, Temple gravely apologised for causing any inconvenience by his unannounced visit. Meanwhile, the old lady nodded affably as if by way of approval.

'My name is Temple—Paul Temple—my card. I wondered if Sir Felix could possibly spare me a few moments.' The old lady carefully wiped her hand on her apron and took Temple's card.

'Why, certainly, sir. I'm sure Sir Felix will be only too pleased,' was the rather surprising reply. 'If you'll just step inside, I'll go and ask Sir Felix.' The studded door swung behind them and they stood in a flagged entrance hall, which was sparsely furnished, and conveyed very little concerning the personal tastes of its owner.

The old lady opened a door on the left.

'If you and the lady will be so kind as to wait in here, sir, I'm sure Sir Felix won't keep you very long.' She closed the door softly behind her, and they heard her footsteps patter away down the hall.

'Well, she's a dear old bird, anyway,' commented Temple, strolling across the room to examine the bookshelves which lined the opposite wall from floor to ceiling.

'What an extraordinary room,' commented Steve, busily taking it in. 'I've never seen so many books together outside a public library.'

'And by Timothy they're beautifully bound,' enthused Temple. 'Must have cost a small fortune.' He ran an appreciative finger along the heavy calf bindings.

'What are they, ancient classics?' asked Steve, who was rather attracted to a corner near the door which housed a case of relics which had obviously been the fruits of Sir Felix's expeditions to Egypt.

'Well, I'm damned!' Steve heard her husband murmur quietly to himself. She swung round.

'What's the matter?'

'They're all detective novels!' he declared, incredulously.

'Don't be silly!' said Steve, going over to the shelves.

'I tell you they are – going right back to Edgar Allan Poe's horror tales! No, wait! Here's a shelf devoted to books on criminology – records of cases ... murder trials ...'

Steve was now scanning row after row of volumes which displayed in gold lettering all the famous names in the world of detective fiction – Dorothy L. Sayers, E. Phillips Oppenheim, Edgar Wallace, Agatha Christie, John Creasey, E. C. Bentley, Dashiell Hammett, Rex Stout, Freeman Wills Croft, Peter Cheyney, John Dickson Carr, and dozens more. It was a paradise for a tired cabinet minister addicted to that type of recreation.

'I don't see any of yours, darling,' said Steve, still scrutinising the shelves.

Temple smiled and said: 'You will, Mrs. Temple, if you raise your head slightly and look a little to the left. They're next to a very peculiar novel called *The Front Page Men*, written by a mysterious lady named Andrea Fortune. I've a suspicion that may be a *nom de plume*.'

'And I have a suspicion that the authoress isn't a hundred miles away at this minute,' came a dry voice from behind them. Steve turned to see an undistinguished-looking man of average height, wearing a plain grey suit, eyeing her quizzically. He was practically bald, and his forehead was smothered with freckles. His complexion was very sallow, as if all the colouring had been etiolated in tropical suns, making him appear much older than he really was.

He came forward as noiselessly as he had entered the room.

'Forgive me if I startled you,' he apologised. His voice had an almost rasping quality.

Steve managed to summon up a reasonable imitation of a gracious smile, and Temple hurried to her rescue.

'Sir Felix Reybourn?' he queried, politely, and on receiving a prompt little nod in reply, continued: 'You probably think this visit a great presumption on our part, Sir Felix, but, well as a matter of fact I'm writing a book—'

'Who isn't?' chuckled Sir Felix, highly amused at his own repartee.

'Quite so,' smiled Temple. 'Mine, however, happens to be a novel about Cairo and the Egyptian desert. Not present-day Cairo, you understand – I want to go back several hundred years, and I thought you might be able to enlighten me on one or two rather important points.'

Sir Felix raised a protesting hand.

'Mr. Temple – please – please! There's positively no reason at all to offer any excuse for this very pleasant informal visit,' the thin voice continued. 'I'm only too delighted to make the acquaintance of yourself and your charming wife.'

72

He paused, then added with the merest suggestion of a chuckle: 'In fact, I have been expecting you, Mr. Temple! Please take that comfortable chair, Mrs. Temple, and my housekeeper will bring some tea immediately.'

And in spite of their protests he insisted on their remaining to tea. Meanwhile, he bustled about, moving an occasional table within reach of Steve's chair, and placing another straight-backed armchair for her husband. 'You'll have to excuse my housekeeper, Mrs. Clarence,' he apologised. 'She's a dear old soul, but hardly as brisk in her movements as she was once, and we are some little distance from the kitchen here. But she has one great asset – she is always ready for visitors – in fact, she welcomes them. So unlike the modern type of servant.'

When at last Sir Felix appeared to have completed his preparations, Temple asked: 'What did you mean, sir, when you said just now that you were expecting us?'

Sir Felix lowered himself luxuriously into his chair, then suddenly focussed a pair of penetrating grey eyes upon the inquirer.

'Mr. Temple, correct me if I am mistaken,' he began in his dry, precise tones, 'but I believe you are engaged in investigating a series of murders committed by an unknown and somewhat melodramatic individual who calls himself The Marquis.'

Feeling a trifle foolish Temple nodded, and Sir Felix went on: 'During the course of your investigations you have hit upon certain salient facts. Briefly, they are as follows: forty-eight hours before Lady Alice Mapleton was murdered, she paid me a visit.'

'That is my information, Sir Felix,' said Temple, seriously. 'I also happen to know that twenty-four hours before the police found the body of Carlton Rodgers—'

'He did me the honour of dining with me,' added Sir Felix, cheerfully. 'Moreover, I believe I was also the last person to see Myron Harwood alive.'

A little puzzled by his complacent attitude, Temple asked: 'Doesn't that strike you as being rather an amazing chain of coincidences, Sir Felix?'

Reybourn did not appear in the least perturbed.

'"Amazing" seems to me almost an understatement, Mr. Temple,' he assented, calmly. 'Why, in plenty of those books yonder, men have been arrested for much less.'

Steve found her voice at last.

'But surely, Sir Felix, you appreciate that all this places you in rather a peculiar position. I'm quite sure that in the face of your admission, ninety-nine out of a hundred people would immediately conclude that you *are* The Marquis.'

Sir Felix permitted himself one of his rare smiles.

'My dear Mrs. Temple, forgive me for saying so, but I am a little disappointed in you. Think now; if I were the elusive individual who seems to be defying the entire personnel of Scotland Yard, do you think I would be quite so stupid as to see Lady Alice Mapleton forty-eight hours before I murdered her? And do you think I would be such an utter nincompoop as to be the last man to see Myron Harwood alive?'

His voice took on an injured tone, but there was the ghost of a twinkle in his grey eyes.

'Now Mrs. Temple – I ask you, is it likely?'

Temple and Steve exchanged an amused smile.

'I see your point,' said Temple, gravely.

Sir Felix rubbed his parchment-like hands.

'I hope so, Mr. Temple, I sincerely hope so. In fact, I knew I would manage to convince you.'

Temple nodded. 'All the same, Sir Felix, if it isn't breaking any confidence, I'd be curious to know why you saw Lady Alice and Harwood and Rodgers at that particular time.'

'Very well, Mr. Temple,' agreed Sir Felix, as Mrs. Clarence bustled in with a large tea tray. 'If it will set your mind at rest, I knew two of these people quite well. Rodgers came to dine on my invitation because I had not seen him since he returned from America three months ago, and I was interested to compare notes with him about certain things – he's a Zoologist too, by the way, or rather he was, poor fellow. Harwood, as you know, is a brilliant scientist, who takes a particular interest in drugs used in bygone ages. He heard I had been making one or two minor discoveries in that direction – I think he read an article of mine in the *Egyptologists' Journal*—so he rang me up and arranged a meeting.'

'Were you able to give him any information?'

Sir Felix shook his head rather wistfully.

'Not very much, I'm afraid. You see, Harwood was a very clever man, and moreover he had a scientist's mind with a passion for formulae. Rather out of my province.'

'And Lady Alice Mapleton?' put in Steve softly, passing him a cup of tea which she had poured out.

'Lady Alice? Ah yes! Lady Alice I had not met before.' He stirred his tea thoroughly. 'I don't know whether I should tell you this, and you must promise to treat it as a confidence.' Upon receiving their assurance, Sir Felix continued: 'Lady Alice came to me because she heard a rumour: she never told me the precise source of her information, but I gather it was picked up at some party in Chelsea. That information concerned a small vessel containing a certain liquid that I had brought back with me on my return from Egypt. Someone had apparently told Lady Alice that the contents of that vessel were a sovereign remedy for breaking the cocaine habit.'

Temple took a deep breath. 'So that was it!' he murmured.

'I'm afraid I couldn't help the poor girl,' Sir Felix went on. 'And I was very upset when I read of her death.'

'You mean you know nothing of the drug you brought back?'

'Very little. To be quite frank, I entrusted it to Myron Harwood, and since his death the small jar seems to have disappeared. I have made exhaustive inquiries of his executor, but he doesn't appear to be able to help me at all.'

'From what I remember,' said Temple, 'you wrote something about those drugs – I happened to come across your article—'

'Oh yes, but my theories were based purely upon local legend; they were in no way scientific. The mixture of drugs was supposed to constitute a very deadly poison the Egyptians called Diamos; a poison that has a most unusual quality. It leaves not the slightest trace in the body of its victim.'

'In fact,' said Temple, 'a very unpleasant weapon to be at large.'

'Extremely unpleasant,' agreed Sir Felix. 'Do try some of that home-made cake, Mrs. Temple. Mrs. Clarence will be mortally offended if you refuse.'

'Are you sure that the poison would still be effective after all these years?' asked Temple with considerable interest. Sir Felix shook his head.

'That is very much open to question,' he replied. 'Harwood was going to make some tests, but he seemed very dubious about reaching any positive results. Of course, the jar was very well sealed, and appeared to be air-tight – but I have every reason to believe it was quite four thousand years old.'

He passed his cup over to Steve to be refilled.

'This has been a most interesting chat,' he declared, 'and I am quite relieved my arguments finally convinced you in face of all the – er, circumstantial evidence. Of course, I was not entirely unprepared. I have to admit that I used the same arguments with similar effect upon a very intelligent young person a short while ago.'

'Indeed?' said Temple.

'Yes, she was a very promising lady detective named, er, let me see …'

'Rita Cartwright?' asked Temple. And Sir Felix nodded.

Strolling through the Mall that evening on his way to the Yard to compare notes with the Chief Commissioner, Temple was busily turning over in his mind the sequence of this amazing series of murders. His work as a writer of detective fiction was responsible for his interest in the machinations of the criminal mind, in which he had developed a rather more penetrative interest than that displayed by the average professional detective.

The Marquis, reflected Temple, certainly had one thing in common with most crooks. He was inordinately vain, as evidenced by his choice of a title, and by his succumbing to the temptation to leave those cards on the bodies of his victims. He was as anxious for his deed to receive maximum publicity as if he were a press agent zealous to snatch a big write-up for some highly-paid film star. With the highly developed scientific resources at the disposal of the Yard, any one of these cards was liable sometime to betray The Marquis' identity. Yet he took a chance, obviously with the utmost self-confidence.

Temple decided that he was probably a man who had got away with other hazards in the past, and had come to the conclusion that he would always be a match for stereotyped police methods. He was bound to make a slip sooner or later. The question was how soon. The public was becoming distinctly alarmed, and certain newspapers were already making ominous comparisons with Jack the Ripper.

While their visit to Sir Felix Reybourn had proved enlightening in some ways, Temple had the uncomfortable feeling that it had opened up several other possible avenues which were irritatingly vague at the moment. Sir Felix was still something of an enigma, and Temple told himself that he would not be surprised to find that the Egyptologist had a closer connection with the case than he would have them believe. He was obviously a man with a considerable brain, and moreover he was tremendously interested in criminology, displaying a wide knowledge of all the latest methods of detection. He would certainly be capable of circumventing these methods.

On his arrival in Forbes' office, Temple was mildly surprised to find one of the visitors' chairs occupied by Roger Storey, whose right arm was in a sling. His coat was torn at the shoulder, and there was a patch of dried mud near his left temple. Inspector Ross was completing a professional-looking bandage round Storey's forearm while Sir Graham looked on.

'Hello Storey,' said Paul Temple, 'what the devil's been happening to you?'

'Quite a lot,' replied Storey, with a rueful smile.

'Things have been happening pretty fast since last night, Temple,' Forbes grimly informed him.

'By Timothy! I can see that!' He crossed over to Storey. 'That arm looks decidedly unpleasant.'

Storey favoured him with a painful grin. 'It isn't exactly my idea of comfort, Mr. Temple, but it might have been much worse.' He eased himself into a more comfortable position as Ross finished the bandage, and turned to Temple.

'Did you manage to see Sir Felix, sir?' he asked.

Temple shrugged a trifle impatiently. 'I saw him all right. But what's been going on here?'

He looked round the small group, noting that each of them seemed to be rather excited.

'I think perhaps you'd better tell Temple all about it yourself, Storey,' suggested Sir Graham.

'Just as you like, sir,' agreed Roger.

'But before you start ...' Forbes turned to Ross. 'Tell Bradley to bring that young man up here again,' he instructed. Ross went out, and when the door had closed, Roger Storey swung round in his chair and half-faced Temple.

'When I saw you last, Mr. Temple, I told you that accidents were always happening to me. I thought at the time that you were inclined to the idea that I was exaggerating.'

Temple shook his head. 'I merely reserved my judgment, Storey, that's all. Sorry if I gave a wrong impression.'

'Well, you can see for yourself I've had another accident today.'

He grimaced as a spasm of pain ran through his arm.

'This morning, I took my car out and went down to Canterbury to visit a relative. I had lunch there and started back in the middle of the afternoon. On the way back, about half-a-mile past the new by-pass road, much the same thing occurred as happened to you and Mrs. Temple on the Embankment the other evening. A car came out of a side-turning and made straight for me.'

He paused and accepted a cigarette which Temple lighted for him.

'Of course, it took me completely by surprise,' he continued, puffing gratefully. 'For a split second I lost my nerve – I didn't know what to do. Luckily, I got a grip on myself before it was too late. I made up my mind like a flash, wrenched at the wheel, swung the car round, and headed for the blighter. I'm getting just about worn out with these "incidents," and I thought I'd settle the issue once and for all. In fact, looking back, I realise now that I was simply seething with rage as soon as it had dawned on me that this was yet another attempt on my life.' Storey's jaw tightened and his eyes seemed to smoulder at the recollection.

'I could see quite clearly that it was a young man driving the other car – a large, six-cylinder Packard. What's more, I could see that I had him on the hop. He hadn't expected any sort of retaliation, and the next we knew was his car had toppled into the ditch, where he had intended to send me. I slammed on my brakes for all I was worth as I shot past him, and as I pulled up I saw him scramble out of his car and make a dash for it. I was pretty badly shaken up, but I was still seething with rage, and I could see it was a case of "now or never." So I went after the swine.'

'Did you catch him?'

'Yes,' replied Storey, a gleam in his eye. 'I caught him all right, but I had to knock him almost unconscious – we had the devil of a scrap. That's how I got this arm so badly knocked about. However, I managed to get him back to the car and brought him straight here.'

'Smart work,' nodded Temple. Storey took out a handkerchief and mopped his forehead.

'I don't mind admitting a few more days like this will finish me,' he declared with some emphasis. Sir Graham passed him half a tumbler of whisky. 'You'll be all right now, Storey. Tell us about this fellow.'

Storey took a gulp at the whisky.

'His name is Slater – Derek Slater,' he told them.

'I've just sent for him, Temple,' put in Forbes, noticing that Storey was still feeling the strain. 'As far as we can gather, he's an actor of sorts. Pretty highly strung at that. I shouldn't think he's more than twenty-two, though he says he's thirty.'

'Will he talk?'

Forbes shook his head. 'Not a syllable. At least, Bradley can't get anything out of him. Whether he's handling the boy right I don't know.'

The door opened to admit the subject of their conversation, escorted by Bradley, who wore a nonplussed expression.

The young man was certainly the unconventional type. His hair was a couple of inches too long in front, and flopped over his eyes from time to time. He affected dark corduroy trousers with a light brown coat and orange hand-woven tie.

Forbes dismissed Bradley, asking Storey to accompany him downstairs and see the police surgeon who had just arrived. When they had gone out, the Chief Commissioner turned to Derek Slater and indicated a chair.

'Sit down Slater,' he commanded, gruffly.

Derek Slater was patently very much overwrought. His lower lip had been bitten until it was bleeding slightly, and there was a wild, desperate look in his eye, such as one might expect from a cornered animal. Temple noticed that a muscle in his face twitched convulsively from time to time. However, he took the chair Forbes indicated without any demur. 'Now Slater,' said Forbes quite kindly. 'Superintendent Bradley tells me you refuse to talk. I wish you'd realise that a little co-operation would greatly benefit yourself, and —'

'I will not stand that third degree stuff,' cried Slater, hysterically. 'If the police can't talk to me reasonably—'

'Now calm yourself, Slater!' begged Sir Graham. 'Nobody's going to put you through third degree. If you'd prefer it, Mr. Temple here will talk to you – and he isn't a policeman.'

Slater looked from one to the other, the hunted expression in his eyes.

At last Temple spoke, quietly. 'Do you know the number of the car you were driving?' he asked.

After a moment's hesitation, Slater nodded.

'It wasn't your car?' hazarded Temple.

Forbes turned to him. 'The car was parked in a car-park just outside Canterbury yesterday afternoon. It was taken there by a girl. So far, we haven't been able to trace her. Slater picked the car up this morning.'

There was a silence. Temple eyed Slater with a thoughtful stare, while Forbes thoughtfully drummed on the desk with his paper-knife.

'Look here,' there was a trace of hysteria in Slater's voice. 'I don't know what all this is about. It was just an ordinary car accident – maybe I was to blame; maybe I wasn't. But I had never set eyes on that other fellow before.'

Temple snapped open his cigarette case.

'Try one of these – it'll quiet your nerves,' he offered. Slater took one and lighted it with shaking hands.

'Now,' said Temple, 'we should be interested to know who told you about this car in the first place.'

Slater hesitated, then suddenly with an impatient gesture he flung his cigarette on the floor. 'Oh for God's sake let me alone!'

Temple walked over and picked up the cigarette which he laid on Forbes' desk. Then he returned to the young man.

'Look here, Slater,' be began, quietly, 'why not lay your cards on the table? You've got to do it sometime.' He placed one foot on another chair and looked down at Slater. 'From the moment I set eyes on you,' he declared, 'I knew you were being blackmailed.'

The young man recoiled visibly.

'It's no ordinary blackmail either,' pursued Temple, evenly. 'However, that's beside the point. *Why* you are being black-mailed is no concern of ours. In fact, we are bleakly disin-terested in that aspect of the case. What we *are* interested in is the man who is doing the blackmailing.'

Slater moistened his lips but did not speak, and Temple continued in a soft voice: 'I refer to The Marquis!'

Disregarding Slater's alarmed expression, he went on persua-sively: 'Now, supposing you stop being a damn fool – and talk!'

But Derek Slater only shook his head, and seemed more frightened than ever. Forbes came over to him.

'Pull yourself together, Slater,' he urged. 'Remember you're under police protection. Nothing can possibly happen to you here.'

Slater still hesitated, as if he were weighing one plan of campaign against an alternative. Finally, he flung back his head with a histrionic gesture, and said in a definite tone:

'All right, I'll tell you as much as I know.'

'I'm sure you won't regret it,' Temple assured him. 'Perhaps you'll tell us from the beginning how you came to be involved – you needn't tell us why you're being blackmailed, of course. That's entirely up to you.'

Derek Slater leaned forward in his chair, and began in a tense voice:

'Almost a fortnight ago, I had a telephone call from a girl. She mentioned the name of the man who has a hold over me, and said that she had been instructed to tell me to go down to Kellaway Manor, near Pevensey Bay in Sussex. When I got there I should receive further instructions.'

'From The Marquis?' interposed Temple, swiftly.

Slater paused, then nodded. 'That was on Friday afternoon,' he continued. 'The following day I went down to Bevensey, and stayed the night at the local inn, The Silver Swan. On Sunday, I set out in search of Kellaway Manor. Nobody at the pub seemed to have heard of the place, and I had the devil of a job in finding it. In fact I nearly gave it up as a bad job. Then a farm labourer put me on the trail.'

He hesitated for a moment, then continued: 'Kellaway Manor turned out to be a derelict sort of mansion on the fringe of a wood, almost fourteen miles from Pevensey. It was a creepy looking sort of place, and seemed to be deserted. The front door bell obviously didn't work, and I knocked for a while without getting any reply. So I decided to walk round the place, and eventually I came to the back door leading into the kitchen. The door was nearly off its hinges, so I entered. It was getting dusk then, but I could see there was a letter on the table. I picked it up and saw it was addressed to me.'

'You mean that was the letter which gave you all the instructions about the Packard and the garage at Canterbury, and the "accident" with Mr. Storey?' queried Temple, a trace of incredulity in his voice.

'I know it sounds like a fairy tale,' said Slater, desperately, 'but I tell you it's true!'

'But this is absurd,' protested Forbes. 'Why didn't he send you the letter in the first place – or get the girl on the phone to give you the instructions?'

'I don't know!' cried Slater more wildly than ever. 'He always works in that cursed roundabout way. I swear to God I'm telling you the truth!'

Forbes shrugged his shoulders dubiously, but made one or two notes. Temple offered Slater another cigarette, as he said: 'Did you recognise the voice of that girl on the phone?'

Slater shook his head.

'Pity,' said Temple, pacing thoughtfully over to the window.

Forbes confronted Derek Slater again.

'Are you really expecting us to believe that the blackmailer had such a hold over you that he could force you into a car collision which might have meant your death?' he persisted.

'It was to have been the last ... settlement,' Slater replied, in a low voice. 'I had to take a chance. In any case life wasn't worth living. I'd have been better off in gaol.'

'Did you keep that letter you found in the kitchen?' asked Temple.

'No. I was told to destroy it immediately: that was in the postscript.'

'How did you destroy it?'

Slater thought for a moment.

'I – I tore it up into little pieces, screwed them into a ball, and threw it into the bushes in the back garden.'

'H'm,' murmured Temple. He turned to Sir Graham.

'Well sir, it looks as if a visit to Kellaway Manor is indicated.'

Slater sprang to his feet.

'No! No! For God's sake keep away from there!' he cried, in agitated tones.

'Why do you say that?' countered Temple, swiftly.

Slater relapsed again.

'I – I don't know. But there's some devil's work going on at that place. I'm sure of it!'

'All the more reason,' said Temple quietly, 'why it should be cleaned up without any delay.'

Slater drew a bewildered hand across his brow in dramatic fashion, but said no more. He was being detained for the night at Scotland Yard, and after Bradley had taken him away, Forbes turned to Temple.

'Temple, you don't think this might be the place we're looking for? You know, the headquarters where The Marquis—' His voice trailed away as he speculated on the possibilities of the theory.

'Well, Temple,' he said at last, arousing himself from his reverie, 'what's your opinion of this Derek Slater business?'

'I think,' replied Temple, suavely, 'that Derek Slater has the makings of a very promising young actor.'

CHAPTER IX

Kellaway Manor

THE offices of Bridley, Taggart and Avery Limited were situated on the second floor of a dignified Victorian building overlooking Cambridge Circus. It would not have been easy to define the exact scope of their business. Their main occupation was the presentation of plays in the West End of London (always providing they could discover the necessary financial backing) but they also conducted a brisk trade as theatrical agents, producers of repertory and touring companies, press agents for theatres and artistes, and publicity and advertising consultants for any type of stage enterprise.

Pete Bridley, the father of the firm, was in retirement now except for a very occasional visit to the office. George Taggart was usually on tour with one or other of the firm's enterprises, and it was left to Dan Avery to hold the fort in the office.

The firm had been responsible for the presentation of Temple's first play, Dan Avery having persuaded a Northern steel merchant that it was worth a gamble. That the gamble failed to materialise any profits did not influence Dan in the least. He pacified his backer – Temple never knew quite how – offered his author one of the famous cigars he kept in his safe, and bade him go and write another play.

He would be a very adamant person who failed to like Dan Avery, and Temple had taken to the brisk little man right from the start of their acquaintance. Dan had turned down his second play in such a pleasant and benevolent manner, that an outsider would have been quite convinced that he was doing the author a very great favour. The play had been eventually produced by another management, and when it had scored a minor success, Dan had been one of the first to congratulate Temple.

However, Dan was quite impressed by Temple's latest play, and had taken an option on it before the novelist sailed for America. Since then, there had been no news, so that Temple decided to pay his sponsor a visit. He knew that Dan arrived at his office promptly at nine-thirty every morning, so he strolled in soon after ten, having arranged to meet Forbes at eleven for their trip to Kellaway Manor.

Already four or five actors and actresses were lounging in Bridley, Taggart and Avery's outer office, eyeing every newcomer with a mixture of intense suspicion and calculated charm. The fact that Temple was immediately ushered into Dan Avery's sanctum created a minor sensation to the accompaniment of raised eyebrows, knowing looks and *sotto voce* comments.

Dan welcomed his visitor with a cheerful smile that was perhaps his greatest asset.

'Why Temple old man, I'd no idea you were back. I've been trying to find out your whereabouts this past three weeks.' This statement was not exactly true, but Temple let it pass.

'Nothing wrong, I hope,' he said, taking the comfortable chair Dan indicated.

'No, no, everything's fine,' replied Dan, quickly. 'I got an offer for the play from Dinmonts.' Temple looked puzzled for a moment.

'But I thought they were a rival firm of yours?'

Dan shrugged.

'My boy, we can't afford to have rivals in this business. If a man comes to me with a good offer, I don't care if he's the Commissioner of Inland Revenue!' He went to the safe and took out the famous box of cigars. Temple tried to refuse one, but Dan pressed it on him. 'Smoke it some other time, my boy, if it's too early now.' He took one himself, carefully cut off the end, and lighted it.

'What's Dinmonts' proposition?' asked Temple.

Dan blew out a cloud of smoke.

'You see it's like this. They've got the Commodore going dark at the end of next month, and they want something to follow *Honourable Lady*. The same sort of thing: intimate comedy with one or two thrills.'

For a little while they discussed the Dinmont contract, then Temple said: 'By the way Dan, did you ever come across an actor named Derek Slater?'

He knew that Avery was a walking 'Who's Who' concerning the theatrical profession and its foibles.

The little man fingered the heavy gold watch chain he always wore across his ample stomach.

'Derek Slater,' he ruminated, 'Yes, I know Derek. He worked for me in the tour of *Love Me Tonight!* Did a lot of work in "rep" before that. I think he was in with that arty crowd at Oxford for a while, you know, a couple of leads and a dozen premium pupils.'

'What d'you know about Slater?' put in Temple, to forestall one of Dan's pet harangues on the subject of amateurs.

'Not a bad actor,' pronounced Dan. 'Not at all bad. Given the right part, he might make a West End name.' He eyed Temple suspiciously.

'Has he been getting at you for the lead in your play?' he demanded. 'Because, if he has I can tell you right away—'

'No, no,' Temple interposed. 'I happened to meet him in a different connection altogether, and I just wondered how reliable he was.'

'Damned unreliable if you ask me,' replied Dan. 'You know what actors are, and he's no better'n any of 'em. And besides...'

He hesitated.

'Yes?' said Temple.

'Mean to say you didn't notice?'

Temple looked at him inquiringly.

'Slater's shot to pieces with dope,' said Dan. 'I thought everybody knew that.'

Temple nodded slowly.

'That's all I want to know,' he murmured.

After a highly indigestible lunch at The Silver Swan, the Scotland Yard contingent, with Temple and Derek Slater, set out for Kellaway Manor. Steve had insisted on accompanying them to Pevensey, but her husband had persuaded her to remain at the inn until they returned. This had not been so difficult as he had anticipated, probably because it was a bleak day in late autumn, with a chill grey mist swirling in from the sea, and the roaring wood fire in the lounge appeared infinitely more attractive than the prospect of a fourteen-mile drive. However, Steve had expressed great disappointment, protesting as always that she was capable of looking after herself.

Derek Slater was much more subdued than in his previous moods and almost inclined to be sullen. He let it be understood that he was being taken to Kellaway Manor against his will, and more than once was heard to declare that he would take no responsibility for the consequences. This had evoked a sharp retort from Forbes, who was immersed in his plan of campaign, and was irritated by the young man's attitude.

The mist seemed to grow thicker when they started, but after the first few miles it cleared a little.

'My God, what weather!' growled Forbes. 'A good job we left Steve at the pub.' He wiped the inside of the wind-screen for the twentieth time without effecting any noticeable improvement. A large lorry suddenly loomed from the mist ahead, and as the police driver rigorously applied his brakes, Temple had visions of another 'accident.' But the lorry slowed down to its left side as it clattered past and vanished in the distance. Soon, they came to a deserted cross-roads with a tilting finger-post, the words being hardly discernible. They turned right at Slater's direction.

'How much farther have we to go?' Temple asked him.

'I don't think it's far now,' he replied, with some hesitation. 'I've only been here once before, and it was all such a nightmare, I can't remember distances very exactly.'

The surface of the road deteriorated considerably, and after a while Forbes told the driver to stop.

'Are we within easy walking distance now?' he asked.

'Oh yes,' replied Slater. 'The road gets very bad – I don't think it would be advisable to take the cars any farther.'

They clambered out and were stretching their stiff limbs as the second police car came to a standstill behind them.

'Is this the place, sir?' asked Bradley, coming up.

'We're just going to investigate,' Forbes replied, his gaze wandering over the long tract of common land, edged by a fair-sized wood. 'Any idea of your bearings now, Slater?' he inquired.

'This mist makes it rather difficult,' replied the young man, whose face wore a worried expression. 'I think the house is about a quarter-of-a-mile away, just beyond the wood. A little further on there is a tall wire fence which runs all round the estate.'

'Humph!' grunted Forbes, suspiciously. 'They've kept that in repair then?'

'Does this road lead right to the house?' asked Temple.

'Oh yes, we go through a gateway when we come to the fence, and then there's a short drive up to the house.'

'Good,' said Forbes. 'We'll go on up – the others can stay this side of the fence.' He gave the necessary instructions, posting the men at hundred yards' intervals along the fence, and stationing a couple of them at the gate. They found this unfastened, and Forbes and Temple went on towards the house itself.

The drive was completely overgrown with grass and weeds, and the house itself seemed to be in no better condition. It proved to be a Victorian mansion of dejected appearance, with wide overhanging eaves and a forbidding ornate iron-work verandah running along its front. Plaster was peeling from the walls, several slates were missing from the roof, and the gardens were a mass of undergrowth. Briars straggled across the overgrown paths, and had even climbed a decayed notice board which stated that 'This desirable Sussex manor house, standing in its own estate of 14 acres,' was for sale by private treaty.

'The gentleman who desires this place must have a very morbid taste,' pronounced Forbes, grimly.

'Oh come, Sir Graham, it's probably very nice in the summer,' smiled Temple, as they edged their way cautiously towards the rear of the building.

Forbes crept up to the kitchen window, his footsteps making no sound in the drenched tangled grass, and peered in through the grimy panes. As far as he could see, it was deserted. The room was very sparsely furnished, had not been cleaned for months, and it seemed as if a tramp or two had found it a convenient billet. Ashes were piled high under the empty grate, the table had a leg missing, there were a couple of decrepit kitchen chairs and two or three newspapers scattered in odd corners.

They went round a corner and pushed open the weather-beaten back door; as Slater had said, it lacked one of its hinges. Forbes rather ostentatiously held a handkerchief to his nose, and with the other hand gripped the butt of his revolver.

'The place is in a filthy condition,' he snorted, making for a door on the far side of the room. This led to a larder which was as bare as Mother Hubbard's proverbial pantry. As Forbes looked in, a rat scuttled to its hole in a distant corner.

'I'll just see what's upstairs,' said Temple, but Forbes caught his arm.

'Wait a minute! I thought I heard someone shouting!'

'You mean outside?'

'Yes, the pantry window's broken.'

They stood listening for a minute or so, then Temple turned towards the staircase.

'While you're up there, see if there's any sign of a telephone,' said Forbes. 'Apparently, the telephone people have been working out this way for some time.'

'That's news to me. How did you know?'

'The landlord at the pub seemed to think that Bradley was the supervisor.'

'Of course,' said Temple, 'they may not have been genuine Post Office engineers.'

'Phew! I wish I'd thought of that – I'd have had it checked.'

'It does seem rather a strange idea to have the phone connected to a place like this just now,' ruminated Temple.

'Not so strange, if the place is being used as we think,' Forbes pointed out.

'Perhaps you're right,' Temple conceded, as he turned to climb the creaking staircase. For the next five minutes, they searched the house very rapidly, but found no trace of any telephone. The place was sparsely furnished, and it looked as if the best pieces of furniture had been removed. Forbes was about to begin tapping the substantial walls in quest of any possible concealed hiding place, when there came the unmistakable sound of two long blasts from a police whistle outside.

Forbes pulled his revolver from his pocket.

'Come on, Temple, we've got to get out of here!' he called. Temple came running downstairs as the whistle sounded again.

'This way,' said Forbes when they stood outside the back door. They hastened to a slope in the ground on the near side of the belt of trees.

Bradley's voice echoed through the mist.

'The fence!' he shouted. 'Keep away from the fence!'

'What the devil!' gasped Forbes, rather winded by his rapid exit.

'Don't touch that fence!' came Bradley's warning shout once again.

'What a damn fool I am!' murmured Temple to himself.

'Eh?'

'They've electrified the fence?'

'Electrified it?' repeated Forbes, in amazement. 'Good God, what's the idea?'

'The idea,' replied Temple grimly, 'is to trap us.'

'But I don't see—'

'To keep us somewhere near the fence,' explained Temple, rather impatiently.

'To keep us somewhere near the fence?' repeated the bewildered Chief Commissioner.

'Don't you see?' cut in Temple urgently. He indicated where a line of fresh soil had been recently turned over. 'They haven't been working on telephone wires; they've been burrowing! In other words, laying a mine!' He hesitated before adding: 'And I'm afraid we're right on top of it!'

For some seconds they regarded each other in silence. A French owl fluttered from one of the trees and hooted drearily at them.

'I believe you're right,' said Forbes at last. 'There must be a power-house somewhere in the wood. That's how they've electrified the fence, and that's how they'll explode the mine if there is one. We've got to get past the fence and find that power-house!'

In less than two minutes they caught sight of the stalwart figure of Bradley.

'There's a hell of a voltage going through this wire, sir,' he announced, harshly. 'Turner happened to be leaning against it when the juice was turned on. He's in a pretty bad way.'

'What about the gate?' asked Forbes, quickly.

'Seems to have some sort of self-locking gadget. It swung to after you entered, and it's locked all right now. Made of iron, too – sure to be alive.'

Sir Graham seemed to be quite at a loss.

'All right, Bradley,' said Temple, quietly. 'Get back up the hill with your men as quickly as you can. Pass the word on to Ross to do the same.'

'Yes ... get a move on, Bradley,' urged Forbes, seeing that Temple had some plan of campaign.

Somewhat mystified, Bradley obeyed.

'Organise a thorough search for that power-house,' Forbes called after his retreating form, and Bradley signalled his assent.

When he had disappeared, Forbes turned to Temple.

'What are you going to do?'

Temple took a neat little revolver from his overcoat pocket.

'This is our only chance, Sir Graham. And there's no time to be lost.'

Forbes eyed the weapon dubiously.

'It's a risk, Temple,' he murmured.

'There's no other way; they should all be out of range now.'

'You'll have to stand well away from it in case it whips back,' he told Temple, who measured his distance carefully and retreated five paces.

The 'crack' and 'ping' seemed almost simultaneous, and a strand of the top wire whistled alarmingly near them.

'Good man!' cried the Chief Commissioner, excitedly.

Once again, Temple took aim and accounted for the middle strand of wire. He was just preparing for the third shot, when there was a faint tremor beneath their feet.

'They've heard the shots!' exclaimed Temple, flinging himself full length on the ground and pulling Forbes with him.

For a moment they both seemed to be engulfed by the reverberating roar and then they experienced the sensation of being picked up by a huge ocean wave and flung helplessly into the air. Fortunately, the soft, mossy turf broke their fall, but they were badly winded, and lay helpless for some seconds while slates, pieces of brick and plaster and odd bits of wood descended all around them. The 'desirable residence' was obviously desirable no longer.

After a while, Temple sat up and gingerly felt his arms and legs, meanwhile surveying the huge crater from which smoke and dust were slowly rising. Temple noticed that they had been flung outside the fence, part of which was uprooted. Sir Graham, who was lying about twenty yards away, rose uncertainly to his feet.

'Are you all right, Temple?' he called.

'I seem to be all in one piece,' replied his companion ruefully, as he noticed a large tear in his overcoat. Forbes went and rescued his hat which was resting on a gorse bush.

'Good job we weren't in that house,' he observed, with a certain amount of grim satisfaction.

Ross and Bradley came running up, and were obviously surprised and relieved to find them uninjured.

'I've got the men spread out, sir,' said Bradley. 'They're patrolling the fence to see if anyone is trying to escape.'

'This fence wasn't electrified when we got here; I'm sure of that,' said Ross. And Bradley agreed.

'If you want my opinion, sir, they planned to watch us with binoculars, but this mist upset their calculations,' argued Bradley. 'They probably had scouts posted to tell them when you and Mr. Temple were on the way to the house, but they had to do the rest by guesswork. They waited a few minutes too long, giving you plenty of time to get settled in.'

'The best thing you can do, Bradley,' interposed Forbes, 'is to call your men together and start a thorough search of that wood. There must be a power-house or apparatus of some sort there. They've probably deserted it now – I expect they made a getaway immediately after the explosion. Mr. Temple and I will go back to the inn.'

Bradley and Ross had begun to move away. Ross suddenly stopped.

'What about Slater, sir?' he asked.

Sir Graham frowned thoughtfully, then decided. 'You can take him with you. Keep a careful eye on him. I'm beginning to think that young man knows quite a lot more than he's told us so far. Report to us as soon as you get back to The Silver Swan.'

When they had gone, Forbes and Temple began to make their way back to the car. They were both beginning to experience a reaction to the exciting events of the past hour. Forbes was limping slightly as a result of a flying piece of timber striking his kneecap, and Temple was battling with a blinding headache.

'I don't trust that fellow Slater,' growled Forbes. 'I'm beginning to think he was put up as a decoy.'

'It certainly looks highly suspicious,' Temple agreed. He chuckled to himself.

'What's the joke?'

'No joke at all, Sir Graham. But one has to admire The Marquis' ambitious outlook. Not many of our master criminals have aspired to blow up half the personnel of Scotland Yard.'

'Humph!' grunted Forbes. 'The devil nearly got away with it too.' As he climbed into his car, a thought struck Forbes.

'Temple, supposing this fellow Slater were The Marquis?'

Temple lighted a cigarette which seemed to relieve his headache a little.

'The theory has its possibilities, Sir Graham,' he conceded. 'I should imagine The Marquis is just the type of person who would plan the wholesale destruction of a group of enemies and go along with them to see that the scheme worked out according to plan. And what's more he'd probably get a considerable kick out of it.'

'Yes,' mused Forbes, 'the more I think of the idea, the more feasible it sounds. I wish we'd brought Slater back with us; I'd like to ask him one or two questions. As it is, there's a chance he might get away.'

'I think Bradley can be relied upon to prevent that,' said Temple.

'M'm ... perhaps you're right,' said Forbes, as he pressed the self-starter, and they began to make their way along the bumpy road. With almost a sigh, Temple settled himself comfortably in his seat.

CHAPTER X

The Marquis Sends a Warning

THE huge logs crackled and spluttered cheerfully in the open fireplace of the lounge at The Silver Swan, throwing a pleasing glow on the dark panelled walls. Steve had established herself in the old-fashioned inglenook, and was looking through a pile of assorted society magazines, most of which were very old and not a little battered. Still, she was enjoying them none the less, for she was so well acquainted with the true stories behind these absurdly glamourised productions which aimed to present the darlings of Mayfair as if they were immortals from Olympus. She knew so well that the more they endeavoured to glorify the Mayfair girl, the more they were threatened with libel actions from all sorts of unexpected quarters.

She turned over pages of wedding photographs, and was chuckling to herself over a picture of 'Lord X and Friend' (she happened to know that the 'friend' had since sued him for substantial breach of promise damages) when she heard a familiar dry rasping voice through the half-open door.

Sir Felix Reybourn popped his head inside the lounge. He was apparently looking for the landlord. When he saw Steve he came over at once.

'Why Mrs. Temple, this is a pleasant surprise!' he cried, and seemed quite genuinely pleased. Steve emerged from the inglenook.

'Hello Sir Felix!' she responded, not a little intrigued at his sudden appearance. 'What are you doing in this part of the world?'

Before Sir Felix could start any explanation, the ample form of his housekeeper filled the doorway. She was very primly clad in a neat black costume and carried a large black bag.

'You know Mrs. Clarence, I think,' smiled Sir Felix.

The housekeeper dropped an old-fashioned curtsey in response to Steve's polite inquiry concerning her health.

'I'm much better than I was, ma'am. I've been suffering with my chest.'

'I'm afraid this mist won't help it very much,' said Steve, sympathetically. 'Won't you come and get warm?'

'Thank ye very much, Mrs. Temple, but I've a little matter to look into for Sir Felix. I'll just pop out and see the landlord.'

'Yes, we haven't very much time, Mrs. Clarence. Perhaps you'll go and find him right away.'

Mrs. Clarence bustled out.

'And mind you look after it!' he called after her. In the doorway, Mrs. Clarence turned and favoured her employer with the merest suggestion of a wink.

When the door had closed, Sir Felix turned and spread his bony hands to the blaze.

'This all sounds very mysterious,' said Steve.

Reybourn's eyes twinkled.

'Ah, the reporter is hot on the scent. Once a newspaper-woman, the old instinct is never quite suppressed, eh Mrs. Temple?'

Steve smiled but did not speak.

'I'm afraid I'll have to disappoint you,' he continued. 'There's practically no mystery at all for you to unravel. Mrs. Clarence is merely exercising her charm to secure me a case of my favourite whisky. I'm afraid I acquired rather a taste for it in Egypt, and the landlord here orders it specially for me. Sorry I can't offer you anything better in the way of a scoop.'

Steve laughed. 'I won't ask you to produce the aforesaid whisky.'

Sir Felix lighted a long, thin cheroot, and sat on the edge of a chair near the fire.

'Well, I've told you my secret, Mrs. Temple. Now perhaps you'll allow me to indulge my curiosity and ask what you are doing at Pevensey?'

'Oh, no,' replied Steve quickly. 'That was originally my question. And I'm still just a little intrigued as to why you should travel all the way from St. John's Wood just to get a case of whisky.'

'But I have a country house in these parts – I suppose you'd call it an estate if you were a house agent. It's about six or seven miles away – Greensea House. I bought it about two years ago. So I'm frequently in this part of the country. I'm sure my friend the landlord will verify this statement. He'll also direct you there if you should feel inclined to drop in to tea one afternoon.'

He flicked his cigar ash into the fire.

'That's my story, Mrs. Temple. Now, how about yours?'

Steve was just wondering how much she should tell Sir Felix when the door opened to admit the inn's solitary waiter.

'I beg your pardon, madam,' said the waiter, 'there's a gentleman to see you. He gave his name as Sergeant Morris.'

She looked surprised, but before she could reply Sir Felix rose to his feet and offered his hand.

'I'll be off, Mrs. Temple. If you're down here for any length of time, don't hesitate to look me up. Mrs. Clarence and I will be delighted to see you. Don't forget – Greensea House – it lies back from the Ashfield Road. The landlord will direct you.'

As Sir Felix tightened his scarf, the waiter whispered in his ear.

'It's in the car, sir, and the lady's waiting.'

Sir Felix smiled. 'Ah yes, thank you Tom.' A coin changed hands. Sir Felix waved farewell to Steve at the door, and when he had gone the waiter said:

'Sergeant Morris is round at the side entrance, madam. If you'll just come through the Smoke Room …'

He led Steve through the low-ceilinged Smoke Room to a doorway in a narrow passage. A thick-set man, with hair slightly greying at the temples, was standing there. He saluted smartly.

'Sergeant Morris?' she asked, in a slightly mystified tone.

'That's right, Mrs. Temple. And this is Detective Gleason.' He indicated a foxy little man who was hovering in the background. Steve decided that she did not like the look of the little man at all, but she reflected that he was probably a very capable detective, and after all few of the Yard men were Adonises.

'What's the trouble, Sergeant?' asked Steve.

'No trouble, madam. Mr. Temple asked us to pick you up and take you to the Keystone cross-roads.' He pointed to a large saloon car which was ticking over just outside the door.

'Is he all right?' demanded Steve anxiously, for she could think of only one reason why her husband should want to see her.

'Yes, he's quite all right, Mrs. Temple,' Detective Gleason assured her. 'It was out of their way to come back here, so we said we'd come and fetch you and drop you at the cross-roads on our way back to Town. I believe Mr. Temple and Sir Graham are going on to dinner somewhere.'

Steve went back for a hat and coat, and presently they were moving swiftly in the direction of the Keystone cross-roads, with Morris at the wheel. Steve was not exactly pleased to find herself sitting in the back of the car with Gleason, but she decided to make the best of it, and tried several times to start a polite conversation. When she inquired about Kellaway Manor, Gleason proved singularly unresponsive, declaring that he had only been 'standing by,' had taken no part in any strategy, and had been prevented by the mist from seeing anything. Moreover, none of his colleagues had had time to tell him what had occurred. It sounded plausible enough.

Steve persisted quietly with an occasional question, for she could not repress a feeling that something was wrong, and that they were trying to withhold bad news from her.

Gleason began to show signs of losing patience, and when after the car had travelled some ten miles, Steve asked: 'Isn't it time we reached the cross-roads?'

He snapped back: 'Keep your mouth shut!' His tone was offensive, and certainly hardly in the best traditions of Scotland Yard. Steve regarded him steadily. A pulse throbbed in her throat, but outwardly she showed no signs of fear.

'Who are you? Where are you taking me?' she demanded.

'You heard what I said,' retorted Gleason, angrily. 'Keep your mouth shut and don't ask any questions.'

'Stop the car!' cried Steve, suddenly flinging herself at Morris, who grabbed the handbrake and wrenched at the wheel as they skidded dangerously round a sharp curve.

'You little devil!' shouted Gleason, pulling her back, and thrusting her roughly into a corner. He held her there while she struggled furiously. He had completely lost his temper now; his face was flushed and a star-shaped scar over his right eye was noticeably inflamed.

'Don't hit her!' gasped Morris, drawing the car into the side of the road. 'Remember our instructions ...'

'We'll have to get rid of her,' panted Gleason.

'Not yet,' said Morris, pressing his foot on the accelerator and quickly changing gear.

Once more Steve flung herself desperately forward, only to be restrained by the perspiring Gleason, who was finding her a considerable handful. A little further on, however, Morris stopped the car.

'O.K. We've done the ten miles,' he announced.

'Thank God for that!' exclaimed Gleason, fumbling in an inside pocket of his coat. Eventually, he produced an envelope and then opened the car door nearest Steve.

'You can find your way back to The Silver Swan quite easily, Mrs. Temple. It's ten miles, and a straight road.'

'What's the meaning of this?' demanded Steve, indignantly. She was more than a little puzzled, for if this were a genuine abduction, why was she being freed at this stage?

'Never mind,' snapped Gleason. 'When you get back, give your husband this letter.' He handed over the envelope.

'And mind you take great care of it,' he nodded.

'Why?'

'Because,' said Gleason, 'it's a letter from The Marquis.' Without any further ado, the car door slammed, the engine roared, and the men who called themselves Morris and Gleason vanished into the mist, leaving Steve standing helplessly in the muddy road, confronted with the singularly unpleasant prospect of a ten miles' walk back to the inn.

On their return to The Silver Swan, Temple made straight for the lounge fully expecting to see his wife surrounded by magazines of all descriptions, for she had announced with some satisfaction that she intended to spend the afternoon in this fashion. But there was no one in the lounge except the waiter carefully distributing fresh ashtrays.

'Have you seen Mrs. Temple, waiter?' he asked. The waiter blinked, as if a little surprised.

'Why yes, sir. She left about three-quarters of an hour ago. Sergeant Morris called for her.'

'What d'you mean – Sergeant Morris?' asked Forbes, who had just entered the room.

'That was the name he gave me, sir,' protested the waiter, 'I was under the impression that he was a – er – plain clothes detective.'

'Oh my God!' breathed Temple, the full significance of the episode striking him. Forbes grasped his arm reassuringly, and turned to the waiter once more.

'What did this man look like?'

The waiter seemed somewhat bewildered. 'Well, he was about your build, sir – rather good-looking,' he began vaguely. 'I believe there was another gentleman with him in a car. Mrs. Temple drove off with them.'

'You don't remember what the second man was like?'

'I didn't take much notice, sir … he was shorter – rather swarthy, I think – but I couldn't be sure.'

Forbes bit his lip, and appeared to be about to ask another question, but he was interrupted by the unexpected entrance of Roger Storey. Storey was obviously excited and he made very little attempt to conceal his emotion.

'What's all the fuss about, Storey?' was Forbes' rather irritable greeting.

'What brings you down here, Storey?' asked Temple.

'I came to see you – and Sir Graham – it's very important—'

Forbes dismissed the waiter.

'Well now, what's the cause of all this?' demanded Forbes, testily.

'I've been worried – hellishly worried,' confessed Storey, sinking into a chair. 'I knew you were coming down here and—'

'How did you find that out?' interposed Temple, swiftly.

'I – er – I happened to overhear a remark at the Yard,' admitted Storey, rather sheepishly. 'And then this morning I discovered that Sir Felix Reybourn had a house near here called Greensea House—'

'And how did you happen to hit on that bit of information?' demanded Temple. Roger smiled, disarmingly.

'It was quite by chance. I wanted to 'phone the garage where I docked my car – it's called the Reindeer Garage – and the name Reybourn happened to catch my eye on the same page of the telephone directory. So I thought I'd come down right away and—'

'Poke your nose into our business, as usual,' snapped Forbes, who was frankly rather bewildered by the rapid developments of the day. 'Let me tell you, Storey, that this business isn't your idea of a party, and we've tolerated your interference long enough—'

'Just a minute, Sir Graham,' Temple interrupted. 'After

all, Mr. Storey has brought us information about this house of Sir Felix Reybourn's.'

He stopped as the waiter came in and looked round uncertainly.

'Would the gentleman mind moving his car, please? The brewer's lorry wants to back over to the cellar and—'

'Certainly,' agreed Roger at once. 'I'll come right away.'

When he had gone, Temple and Forbes regarded each other in silence for some moments.

'That's a queer bird. I can't quite fathom him,' admitted Forbes, presently. 'Outwardly, he's just one of those damned playboys with a sight too much money. Yet he always manages to come on the scene at awkward moments!'

Forbes rammed a charge of tobacco into his pipe.

'D'you think it's true about Sir Felix?' he demanded, gruffly.

Temple shook his head. His brain was still busy on the problem of the two men in the car.

'If it is,' pursued Forbes, playing with the idea, 'if it is true, then it explains a good deal.'

But Temple was obviously far more worried about what had become of Steve. She was constantly assuring him that she could look after herself, as she had done in her newspaper days, and she was never tired of reminding him of the occasion when she had been confronted by a certain 'Catty' Larrabie, a desperate criminal who had eluded Scotland Yard for seven weeks after his escape from Pentonville. Following a remote clue, Steve had run Catty to earth just outside a deserted dock in the East End. Something in his eye told her that he was just as scared as herself, so she calmly offered him a cigarette, then one of the sandwiches she had with her. Catty had almost dissolved into tears, and provided Steve with a front page scoop that was the talk of Fleet Street for months.

But this was a long time ago, and present realities invariably appear more terrifying than past dangers. Temple fumed at himself for under-estimating The Marquis' organisation, which was apparently equal to leading himself and Sir Graham into a trap and simultaneously kidnapping his wife. Furthermore, it was obviously an organisation that was relentless as it was calculating.

Pulling at his briar, Forbes was brooding upon similar lines. He was debating upon the most advisable course of action, and decided eventually that he must await the return of Ross and Bradley with his men, when some rather more extensive operation might be possible.

Temple paced distractedly up and down the lounge.

'Have you anyone named Sergeant Morris at the Yard?' he asked.

'Yes,' said Forbes, 'as a matter of fact, we have. But he doesn't answer to the waiter's description, and furthermore, he's busy on that suicide job at King's Langley. He wouldn't come down here with a cock and bull yarn of that description. No, we've got to face it, Temple. They were a couple of The Marquis' men, and we've got to get after them just as soon as Ross and Bradley—'

He broke off and ran to the window as a car drew up outside, followed by another. A car door opened, and, imagining he heard a familiar voice, Temple crossed to the window. His ears had not misled him. Steve was calmly descending from the first car, chatting to Ross and Bradley. He rushed outside like a man possessed, and met Steve as she was just about to enter.

'Hello, darling,' she welcomed him. 'Are you pleased to see me?'

'What's all this about, Ross?' asked Forbes when the

Inspector came in. 'Are you anything to do with this mysterious Sergeant who called for Mrs. Temple?'

'No sir,' replied Ross, in an injured tone. 'We picked up Mrs. Temple about eight miles away. She was walking. Seems a couple of damn fools passed themselves off as Scotland Yard men, took her out in a car and more or less dumped her, so far as I can gather. I can't quite fathom what they were up to—'

'Did you know them, Steve?' asked Forbes.

'No – but I'd recognise them anywhere.'

'Can't you recall anything outstanding?'

'Why yes – the one man who called himself Gleason had a star-shaped scar over his right eye.'

'Was he a little man with a foxy sort of face and ginger-brown hair?' interposed Bradley quickly.

'Why yes – that's the man.'

'Sounds like Lannie Dukes,' said Bradley. 'Perhaps you'll come round to the Yard when we get back, Mrs. Temple, and I'll show you some photographs of him.'

'Why of course, Inspector,' she readily agreed.

'What else happened, Steve?' demanded Temple, anxiously.

'Nothing very much, darling. They just took me ten miles, then handed me a letter and left me. The letter's for you, by the way. I hope you don't mind my opening it – you know I never open your letters as a rule. But the circumstances were a little unusual.'

She was about to hand it to Temple, when Bradley restrained her.

'Just a minute, Mrs. Temple. There may be some useful fingerprints on that envelope.'

Steve shook her head. 'I don't think so. I noticed the little man handled it with washleather gloves, and I expect whoever wrote it did the same.'

Temple took the letter and held it by the extreme top left-hand corner. Although it was only a brief note, he scanned it thoughtfully for two or three minutes.

'What's it say?' asked Forbes at last, unable to restrain his curiosity any longer. Temple read aloud:

Next time will be different; but there will be no next time, Mr. Temple, if you are wise and do not interfere. The Marquis.

'Let Bradley have it, will you, Temple?' asked Forbes, and the Superintendent produced a pair of tweezers, with which he transferred the letter to his wallet.

'Did you find that power-house, Ross?' asked Sir Graham, anxious to formulate some plan of campaign. Ross nodded.

'Yes sir, Bradley and his men found it. It was a converted summer house in the wood – about a quarter-of-a-mile away.'

'Anyone there?'

'No, sir. Quite deserted, and all the power cut off. The dynamo was still warm.'

'Humph!' said Forbes. 'Any fingerprints?'

'Not a sign, sir,' replied Bradley. 'I imagine they were all wearing rubber gloves. I've left a couple of men there to comb the place over, but I doubt if they'll find anything.'

Steve drew her husband towards her and whispered:

'Darling, did you know that Sir Felix Reybourn has a house down here?'

'Why yes,' he smiled. 'Mr. Storey came down specially from Town to tell us.'

'Storey?' she seemed startled.

'That's right, darling. Now, if you're not too tired after all your hiking, perhaps you'll run and put on your best bib and tucker—'

'Darling, you don't mean we're going out again?'

'I'm afraid so, darling. It really is rather important.'

'But where on earth ...'

'To yet another desirable country mansion ... Greensea House!'

CHAPTER XI

Greensea House

FORBES and Temple began to make plans immediately. It was decided that Steve and her husband should be accompanied by Forbes, Ross, Bradley and the inevitable Storey, all travelling in the largest of the cars which would accommodate the entire party. After some discussion, Sir Graham agreed it was best that Temple and Steve should visit the house alone, the others remaining within easy call. As Steve pointed out, Sir Felix had invited her to drop in at any time. On the other hand, the presence of police officers would most certainly put Sir Felix on his guard and possibly close all future avenues of approach, whether the visit proved fruitless or not. So it was agreed that Temple should carry a police whistle in case of extreme emergency, and the Yard men would be within earshot.

Following the landlord's directions, they had little difficulty in finding Greensea House before dusk fell. The name was painted on the large gates at the entrance, and Forbes steered the car on to the grass verge at the side of the road under some overhanging trees. As the engine wheezed into silence, the Chief Commissioner asked:

'Have you decided what you're going to say to Sir Felix?'

'Yes,' amplified Storey. 'You can't just mention casually that you've dropped in for a cup of tea.' He was doing his best to be helpful, for he felt that his presence was not altogether welcome. In fact, he had had to exert considerable persuasive powers to cajole Forbes into allowing him to join the party.

'On the other hand,' said Steve, 'we can't ask Sir Felix if his house happens to be The Marquis' headquarters.'

'Leave it to me,' said Temple, 'I daresay I'll think of something.'

'All the same, Steve,' declared Sir Graham, with some emphasis, 'if you as much as set eyes on one of those men who came for you this afternoon, give Temple the tip right away, and I'll have a warrant out for Sir Felix immediately.'

They got out of the car and began to look round. There was a nip of frost in the air, and the moon was rising above the mist, giving it a strange luminous quality. It was almost dark now, but they could just discern the shadowy outline of the house through the trees.

'Pretty impressive-looking place,' commented Forbes. 'Sir Felix must have a hefty income to keep two large houses going. I didn't know Egyptology paid such good dividends.'

'Baronets do occasionally inherit money with their title,' Temple reminded him.

'H'm, yes, I suppose so. Oh well, better be moving. We'll get behind those laurels in the drive and keep out of sight. Mr. and Mrs. Temple will walk up the drive in the ordinary way.'

'Give us a quarter-of-an-hour, Sir Graham,' said Temple, 'then if you don't hear from us ...'

'We'll storm the bastille!' said Roger.

'Righto,' laughed Temple. 'Though on second thoughts, you'd better make it twenty minutes – the drive seems a fair length, and it'll probably take an extra five minutes before we – er – make contact.'

'Twenty minutes then,' promised Forbes. 'Good luck!'

Paul Temple and Steve set off at a brisk pace in the direction of the house. The mist was patchy, but they managed to find their way to the front door without making use of their torch. Finally, they had to use it, however, in an effort to discover the bell.

During their search, they heard a sound which caused Steve to pause for a moment and grip Temple's arm: through the stillness of the evening came the strange eerie howling of a bloodhound. It began with a deep bay, and ended on a prolonged wailing note.

'We seem to have been provided with appropriate sound effects,' commented Temple, and Steve forced a smile.

They listened in silence. After a few minutes, the noise stopped, and Temple turned his attention to the door again. The narrowly-focussed beam from the electric torch flickered across the front of the house.

'There doesn't seem to be a knocker, only a letter-box,' he whispered. Neither was there any sign of a bell. Temple was about to rattle the letter-box and in doing so he pressed against the door.

'By Timothy! It's open!' he exclaimed in surprise.

He was pushing it open wider, but Steve laid a hand on his arm.

'Darling – we can't go in,' she breathed.

'Keep your torch handy,' he replied, 'and don't be scared, Steve!'

'Paul, do be careful!'

Temple took Steve's arm, and focussing the torch ahead, they advanced slowly into the stone-flagged hall; a grandfather clock ticked with measured beat and a slight clanking of the pendulum sounded almost deafening in the intense silence.

'I'm sure we shouldn't—' Steve was starting to protest, when Temple interrupted her by calling out: 'Hello there! Anybody at home?'

His voice died abruptly into echoes.

'H'm, it seems deserted,' he murmured.

'Don't you think we ought to get back to Sir Graham and—'

'All right,' he agreed, 'we'll just take a look in here first.' He opened a door on the left and swept his torch round the room. It was furnished in very much the style Temple had expected. There were several Hepplewhite chairs and a quaint writing bureau in the far corner.

'Empty,' he pronounced, laconically. 'Looks like the morning room.'

'What a lovely old coffee set in that cupboard,' said Steve. 'I'm sure it's Wedgwood.'

'Speaking as an interested layman, I should say you were right.'

Temple crossed the room, leaving Steve standing somewhere near the door. He was moving very silently on rubber-soled shoes, and had switched off his torch. The moon was shining through one of the windows, lighting up one corner as its beams came obliquely across the room, throwing the rest of it into rather more intense shadow.

'Don't do that, darling, you made me jump,' said Steve, suddenly. She had her back to the room, and was trying to examine the corner cupboard.

Temple looked round in surprise.

'What d'you mean?' he asked.

'You touched my hand, dear.'

Temple made an involuntary movement.

'I could hardly have done that when I was over here, quite ten feet away.'

'But you're touching it now,' protested Steve, from the gloomy corner where she was standing.

Temple swung the torch full on her, and had some difficulty in restraining a gasp.

'For God's sake don't move!' he breathed.

'What is it? Paul, what is it?'

'Don't move, Steve! Don't move!' he repeated, in even tones. He was trying not to alarm her. He half-turned away from her, took out his automatic and aimed very carefully at two beady eyes in the V-shaped head of the snake which was sliding over the arm of a chair.

Steve watched in terrific fascination. The snake withdrew its head suddenly, and Temple had to move to a fresh position. The light of the torch seemed to dazzle the reptile. He was taking careful aim again when the room was suddenly flooded with light, and Temple swung round abruptly. At the door stood Sir Felix Reybourn, with Mrs. Clarence hovering in the background.

'Oh dear, it's that Tina again!' said the housekeeper, in some annoyance. She crossed over towards the snake, which vanished under a sofa.

'It's all right, Mrs. Temple,' said Reybourn reassuringly. 'Tina is quite harmless, though she *will* roam about in awkward places!'

With a smile Temple replaced his automatic pistol.

'Now come along, Tina,' admonished Mrs. Clarence. She began making soothing noises, and eventually ran the reptile to earth in a corner, where – to Steve's bewilderment – she calmly picked it up and carried the snake out of the room.

Open-mouthed, Steve watched her, and when she had gone, sighed audibly in relief.

'I'm sorry if Tina upset you, Mrs. Temple,' Sir Felix apologised. 'I keep a lot of pets, you know, down here. Most of them are quite harmless, but perhaps a little terrifying.'

'Surely she's a viper,' said Temple.

'Oh yes – one of the most dangerous till her fangs were extracted. But she's amazingly tame nowadays. Sensitive too. I daresay she was just as scared as you were!' He laughed somewhat deprecatingly.

'By jove, you must think me quite a character! I'm a zoologist in my spare time, you know, Mrs. Temple, so that accounts for the strange collection of friends. Shall we go into the drawing-room? There's a fire in there.'

He led the way, letting them pass out of the room before him. As he paused at the door to switch off the light, a thought obviously occurred to him.

'Oh Mr. Temple, forgive my asking, but how did you manage to get into the house?'

Somewhat taken aback, Temple hesitated, and it was left to Steve to fill the breach. She smiled disarmingly.

'It was very presumptuous of us, Sir Felix, but the front door was partly open, and we couldn't make anyone hear.'

'Open?' repeated Reybourn, in surprise. 'Are you sure?'

'Of course,' said Temple. 'See – it's still open—'

Sir Felix crossed to the door, peered out for a moment, then closed it.

'That's very extraordinary. I don't see how it could have happened.'

'Have you been away from the house very long?'

'Yes, it must be at least an hour and a half,' calculated Sir Felix, thoughtfully. 'After we left you at the inn, Mrs. Temple, we came straight back here, then we went on to Ferndale Court, Lord Breckton's place. He's an old crony of mine, who lives about half-a-mile away. We left there about – well – fifteen minutes ago I should think.'

'I suppose Lord Breckton could verify that,' suggested Temple. Reybourn seemed faintly annoyed.

'Of course he could verify it – if you consider that necessary,' he replied, rather petulantly.

'It may be necessary,' answered Temple, slowly.

'What d'you mean?' demanded Reybourn, the colour mounting to his sallow features.

Temple pointed to a dark, moist stain that was visible near the door.

Reybourn stooped and examined it. He touched it with his finger then slowly recoiled.

'Good God, it's blood!' he cried. There was no mistaking the panic in his voice. 'But – but how could blood get there?'

Temple leaned against an antique oak chest.

'Now Sir Felix, let us be quite honest with each other. What does that suggest to you?'

Sir Felix's brow was corrugated in deep thought.

'Well,' he said at last, 'it looks to me as if someone has been badly hurt and then taken through the front door and out of the house.'

'Just so,' Temple nodded. He paused before adding as he looked full into Reybourn's eyes: 'Did *you* take anyone out of the house tonight, Sir Felix?'

The Egyptologist backed in alarm.

'No! No! I swear I never—'

He was interrupted by a sudden shriek, which was repeated almost immediately. Then there was a sound of footsteps, a door was flung open and Mrs. Clarence came rushing into the hall in a state of great agitation.

'Sir Felix!' she screamed.

'My dear Mrs. Clarence, whatever's the matter?' He went over and supported her.

'I – I – was drawing the curtains in the library,' she panted, 'and … and …'

'Easy now, Mrs. Clarence. Take your time!'

'I must be seeing things, Sir Felix!' she gasped.

'Please tell us what you saw, Mrs. Clarence,' urged Temple.

She clutched a corner of her apron.

'I happened to look through the library window. It's bright moonlight outside now, and … oh, Sir Felix, there's a *body* out there!'

She collapsed into hysterics.

'Look after her, Steve,' said Temple, quickly. 'Come on, Sir Felix – which is the best way?'

'Through the front door – it's only round the bend!'

In a few seconds they were standing beneath the library window.

The man was lying face downwards.

'Poor devil,' murmured Reybourn, 'Is he …?'

Temple stooped. 'Yes, I'm afraid so,' he presently announced.

'Oh, my God,' said Reybourn softly.

Temple switched his torch full on the features of the dead man.

'Have you seen this man before, Sir Felix?'

'No – honestly I haven't,' replied the other, in earnest tones. 'I've never set eyes on him in my life.' He seemed very upset, but presently asked: 'Have you any idea who he is, Mr. Temple?'

'I have,' said Temple shortly.

He switched off the torch.

'His name is Derek Slater.'

CHAPTER XII

Accidental Death?

SIR GRAHAM FORBES toyed with a bright new puce folder which was labelled 'Derek Slater,' opened it and ran through its meagre contents for the tenth time. They consisted of Slater's statement, which had been typed out and signed, a few rough notes taken by Sir Graham and Bradley, a letter from a theatrical manager which was in Slater's wallet, and finally the inevitable card with its inscription in purple ink, which had been discovered in Slater's vest pocket.

Paul Temple sat on one arm of a chair, absorbed in *The Daily Record Literary Supplement*, where his latest novel was far too briefly reviewed for his liking. True, the last five chapters had been written almost entirely on the outward trip to America in less than a fortnight in order to fulfil a promise to his publisher, yet Temple felt that it merited rather more than half-a-dozen lines of cynically written synopsis of the plot.

He passed on to the painfully prolix reviews of books written by politicians, newspaper-men and refugees. Finally, he tossed the paper aside and began an irritating argument with Sir Graham concerning the death of Derek Slater.

Temple persisted that although the case against Sir Felix Reybourn appeared conclusive, it was all just a little too cut and dried, as if it had been contrived very deliberately by an enemy who was planning Sir Felix's downfall. Forbes became more and more annoyed, until he finally closed his folder and banged it with his fist.

'I can't see it at all, Temple. You're barking up the wrong tree altogether.'

'I suggest you smoke one of your excellent cigars,' suggested Temple, equably. 'It will give you a mellower outlook on life in general, and you'll realise that poor Sir Felix is just an innocent victim of a master mind.'

'Dammit man, this isn't one of your detective novels,' broke in Forbes, testily.

Temple picked up his paper and folded it carefully, a faraway look in his eyes. 'D'you mind if I try one of your cigars?'

Forbes pushed the box towards him.

'That's your trouble, Temple, if you don't mind my saying so. You've got the fiction writer's outlook. Because suspicion falls heavily on Sir Felix, you leap to the conclusion automatically that he's innocent. It won't do, you know, Temple. You have only to read the papers to see that these things don't happen once in a hundred cases.'

Temple drew a luxurious mouthful of smoke from his cigar.

'These are even better than pre-war, Sir Graham,' he declared, inconsequently. 'Really, I'm amazed!'

Forbes made an impatient gesture.

'I've given this matter a great deal of thought, Temple, and it's my contention that Sir Felix Reybourn is The Marquis.'

'Then,' said Temple, puffing a neat ring of blue smoke into the air, 'why don't you arrest him, Sir Graham?'

'I have already issued a warrant,' replied Forbes. Temple dropped his paper, and for the first time since his arrival at the Yard seemed really interested in the proceedings.

'I sent Bradley down to Pevensey first thing this morning,' continued Forbes. 'He had a warrant on a charge of murdering Derek Slater.'

'For the murder of Derek Slater?' repeated Temple, incredulously.

'And why not?' snapped Forbes. 'Good God man, whether Reybourn is The Marquis or not, you're not going to tell me he didn't murder Derek Slater!'

Inspector Ross looked up from a report he was writing at a desk in a distant corner.

'He murdered Slater all right; there's nothing more certain,' he declared, confidently.

Temple turned to the speaker.

'Really, Inspector?' he murmured suavely. 'What makes you think so?'

Ross propped his chin on his hand.

'Oh come now, Mr. Temple,' he expostulated. 'In the first place, after you and Sir Graham left Kellaway Manor, the rest of us made a search for the power-house in the wood. When we found the place, it was deserted.'

'Well?' said Temple.

'During that search – it was pretty foggy remember – we lost Slater.'

'Good God!' cried Temple. 'Why didn't you say so when you got back?'

'We didn't get much chance – with all that scare about Mrs. Temple's abduction, and making plans to go to Reybourn's,' Ross reminded him. 'Bradley and I have been on the carpet about it,' he declared ruefully with a glance at Sir Graham, 'but we took it for granted that the poor devil had got the wind up and gone back to Town. What actually happened, however, is pretty obvious.'

'Then supposing you tell us what actually happened,' Temple suggested.

'Well, sir, in my opinion, Sir Felix was in the power-house. He had plenty of time to get there after leaving The Silver Swan. After the mine went off, he made a dash for it, and by accident or design bumped into Slater. He may have ordered him to go to the powerhouse – or perhaps Slater merely ran in that direction by chance. Reybourn knocked Slater out, bundled him into his car and took him back to Greensea House.'

'Wouldn't it be rather an exertion for an old gentleman to carry an unconscious man all that way?'

'He'd probably got confederates,' replied Ross. 'Until it got dark, the body was kept indoors at Greensea House, then with a bit of help from Mrs. Clarence – or whoever was around – the body was dumped in the shrubbery. It's my contention that they were actually doing this when you and Mrs. Temple arrived.'

'H'm ...' murmured Temple, non-committally, but Forbes was more enthusiastic.

'I agree, Ross! I agree one hundred per cent!'

'You see, Mr. Temple,' pursued Ross, gaining more confidence. 'It fits together like a jig-saw puzzle.'

'I've a feeling you're going to have some bits left over,' mused Temple. 'Still, carry on, Inspector.'

'When you and Mrs. Temple arrived, the door was open,' went on Ross. 'If Sir Felix and Mrs. Clarence were at the back of the house, as I suspect, then they'd be likely to leave the door open. It would be, more or less, a natural thing to do.'

'Yes, but just a minute, Ross,' interposed the Chief Commissioner. 'We've checked up that alibi. Both Sir Felix and Mrs. Clarence were at Lord Breckton's place till six-thirty.'

Ross was momentarily nonplussed.

'If I might suggest an alternative theory,' put in Temple, diffidently. 'Supposing Ross to be right, and that the person escaping from the power-house bumped into Slater and knocked him out. Now assume that this person was not Sir Felix, but someone who wanted to throw suspicion – or shall we say continue to throw suspicion – on to Sir Felix.'

Forbes looked up sharply.

'What then?' he asked curiously.

'Well now, they'd take Slater to Greensea House, and when they found the place empty – Sir Felix and Mrs. Clarence being at Lord Breckton's – they'd open the front door with a skeleton key and dump Slater in the hall.'

'But he was found in the shrubbery.'

'Of course he was! For the simple reason that when Slater was left at the house, he wasn't dead. He managed to get up and open the front door. Instinctively, he left it open, and then staggered out into the drive. It was getting dark. The poor devil was frightened, and would hardly know what he was doing. He stumbled round the side of the house, and fell into the shrubbery.'

'M'm,' nodded Forbes. 'An interesting theory at any rate.'

But Ross was frankly sceptical.

'Aren't you stretching it a bit, Mr. Temple, when you jump to the conclusion that Slater could get into Sir Felix's house as easily as all that?'

'Why not? If he hadn't a skeleton key, he might even have had a pass key. A man who was out to throw suspicion consistently upon Sir Felix might be expected to go to considerable trouble to obtain a duplicate of all his keys. They would be practically indispensable to such a person,' insisted Temple.

Forbes laughed. 'No, no, Temple! You'd better go and write a novel about it. That's the best thing you can do with that idea, and it's about all your theory's good for.'

'There's only one person with a key to Greensea House,' declared Ross, dogmatically, 'and that is Sir Felix himself. I'm absolutely convinced he's the man who murdered Slater.'

Temple shrugged.

'Well, I'm delighted to hear you say that, Inspector. There's nothing I like better than to hear a man say he's absolutely convinced about something.' He paused, then continued in a detached sort of voice. 'So Sir Felix left the power-house, bumped into Slater, knocked him out, and, instead of leaving him in the wood, took him all the way back to Greensea House, and more or less dumped him at his *own* front door.'

He turned to Forbes.

'If I wrote *that* story, Sir Graham, I've a feeling I'd have some difficulty in finding a publisher!'

A sergeant interrupted them with the news that Roger Storey was outside waiting to see Temple.

'We'll have him in here, if you don't mind, Sir Graham. He may have stumbled on another piece of information,' said Temple. Forbes agreed, and a few seconds later Roger entered.

With his arm slung in a black silk scarf, the young man seemed to have regained some of his old nonchalance. He came in briskly, nodded to Ross and smiled engagingly at Forbes and Temple, who could not help noticing that he wore an extremely well-fitting suit, which looked as if it had only just left the tailors. Indeed, Temple could recall that Storey had worn three other suits since they first met – all of them of an expensive material and cut. There seemed to be no limitations to the young man's wardrobe.

He appeared to be supremely conscious that he was well-dressed, and he came across to Forbes' desk.

'I do hope I'm not making a nuisance of myself, Sir Graham,' he apologised.

'You look much better, Storey,' said Temple. 'And you almost tempt me to ask you to divulge the name of your tailor.'

'As long as you don't ask me to divulge how much I owe him,' Storey grinned.

Forbes eyed the young man keenly.

'I gather you want a word with Temple alone,' he said, rising from his chair, But Storey held up his hand.

'No, no – please Sir Graham. You must all stay. I did try and get you on the telephone, Temple, but your man said you were here. So I thought there was no time to be lost ...'

With his free hand he was extracting a letter from an awkwardly placed inside pocket. 'This will explain the reason why I'm in such a hurry.' He handed over the letter to Temple, who opened it and read:

The Hon. Charles Serflane,
284B Park Lane, W1

Dear Sir,
I have in my possession four letters which were
written by you to Miss Laraine Curtis on August 7th,
10th, 14th and 17th of last year. It is my opinion
that these letters are worth precisely seven thousand
pounds, and I would suggest, therefore, that you take
the necessary steps to secure this amount. Having
done so, put the money in a small leather suitcase,

*and hand it over to a young lady who will meet you
at the entrance to Oxford Circus tube station
tomorrow evening at six-thirty. It is imperative that
you carry out these instructions personally.*

The Marquis.

Temple passed on the letter to Forbes, who read it and handed
it to Ross. 'When did this arrive?' asked Temple.

'Yesterday morning,' replied Storey. 'The poor devil was
in the hell of a state. Didn't know which way to turn, and
in desperation he came to me.'

'Why?' asked Ross in a puzzled voice. 'Why didn't he
come to Scotland Yard?'

'Because he was frightened. The very thought of a scandal
has nearly given him heart failure. He doesn't stand too well
with his people at the moment – they haven't forgotten his
flutter with the Curtis girl – and he daren't risk anything
like this coming out.' He hesitated, then added by way
of explanation: 'You see, Charles and I were at Oxford
together.'

Forbes traced patterns on his blotter with his paper-knife.

'This Laraine Curtis,' he said, 'who is she?'

'One of the show girls at The Highstepper Club. Charles
was crazy on her for a while, but the affair cooled off. I've
already 'phoned her about the letters.'

'What did she say?'

'Apparently, they were stolen from her flat. Nothing else
was missing, so she decided she wouldn't make a fuss about
it, for Charles' sake. She was quite fond of him, you see.'

'H'm,' mused Forbes. 'I suppose it is possible.' But the
tone in which he spoke was more than a trifle sceptical. 'You

don't think she's mixed up in this affair, Storey? Could she have any connection with The Marquis?'

'It's possible of course,' conceded Roger. 'She's a typical hard-boiled Cabaret girl who mixes with all sorts of men as long as they pay the bill. But the last I heard she was engaged to get married.'

'It doesn't sound as if she'd be interested in blackmail at this stage,' said Ross. 'Those girls get a tenner a week and most of their meals cost them nothing.'

Temple, who had been carefully examining the envelope, told them that the letter had been posted at Wimbledon.

'That's my part of the world,' said Ross, glancing up from the report he was still writing. 'Look well if the blighter's living on my doorstep.'

'Wimbledon's a fair-sized place,' said Temple.

Ross grinned. 'Don't I know it! I patrolled every blessed back alley for over seven years. Most people outside Wimbledon seem to think it's just a dozen tennis courts.'

Forbes turned to Storey.

'When are you seeing Serflane?' he asked.

'This morning, Sir Graham. We're lunching together.'

The Chief Commissioner thoughtfully stroked his chin.

'All right. Tell him not to worry – we'll be looking after him. He must do exactly as the letter says.' He ignored Storey's surprised exclamation. 'It doesn't matter about the seven thousand – he can use an empty suitcase, but he must meet the girl. That's absolutely essential! You understand that, Storey?'

'Yes, Sir Graham.'

Forbes turned to Ross. 'Our best plan would be for you to take half-a-dozen men,' he decided. 'And you may as well pick up Serflane on the way there, so's you can identify him. But keep well out of sight in the tube.'

He was interrupted by the sudden entrance of Superintendent Bradley.

'You've been quick, Bradley,' said Forbes, rather mystified. 'Is anything the matter? Did you get Sir Felix all right?'

Bradley hesitated for a moment, obviously excited.

'He'd left with Mrs. Clarence before I got there,' he announced.

'You mean you've lost them?'

Bradley shook his head. 'They left Pevensey by road soon after nine o'clock. Just outside Barking, the car skidded and overturned.'

'Phew!' whistled Ross.

'Mrs. Clarence was only shaken, it was an absolute miracle,' Bradley continued. There was a pause, then Forbes asked: 'And Sir Felix?'

'Sir Felix,' said Bradley, deliberately, 'is dead.'

The men looked at each other.

'My God, I don't believe it!' said Roger at last.

'Who identified the body?' asked Forbes.

There was yet another pause before Bradley said: 'I did, Sir Graham!'

CHAPTER XIII

Paul Temple Keeps an Appointment

PAUL TEMPLE was strangely restless for the remainder of the day. He insisted upon taking Steve to lunch, and in the ornately decorated dining-room of the Cosmopolitan Grill he told her that there was an idea seething in his brain, and that he felt sure that noise would prove the right accompaniment to its satisfactory development.

'But darling, how can you possibly think in the midst of all this noise?' protested the bewildered Steve.

'In your newspaper days,' he reminded her, 'you told me you often wrote your stuff with the telephones buzzing, subeditors rushing about, and boys screaming for copy.'

'Yes, but you wouldn't exactly call that creative work,' she pointed out.

'Don't argue with me, darling,' he pleaded. 'Just eat and agree with me if I make a remark that seems not quite sane. And now let's gossip for all we're worth – the same as everyone else. Tell me, what have you been doing this morning?'

Steve smiled as she said: 'I went to Scotland Yard.'

He looked up quizzically.

'Oh – why Scotland Yard?'

'You remember, darling. Superintendent Bradley asked me to call and look at some photographs of that man Gleason.'

'Ah, yes! Was he the man they suspected?'

She nodded.

'Yes – he was Lannie Dukes all right, but according to Bradley, he seems to have disappeared. Ross has been looking for him for some days, but after the raid on that house in Bombay Road he appears to have vanished from all his regular haunts.'

'Oh well,' said Temple, frowning over the menu, 'I daresay it's only a matter of time ...'

After he had ordered lunch, Steve suddenly leaned forward and said: 'Paul – you didn't tell me about Sir Felix.'

'Then who did?'

'Superintendent Bradley.'

Somewhat abruptly Temple said: 'Don't go upsetting yourself, Steve.'

'But darling, Sir Felix seemed such a harmless old man.'

'Forbes has a strong suspicion that he's The Marquis. At any rate, he's quite certain he murdered Slater.'

'Murdered Slater?' Steve echoed incredulously, for she had begun to acquire a liking for Sir Felix, with his dry, rasping voice, charming manners, and quaint sense of humour. 'Surely, if he were a murderer, he'd have killed us long ago – or tried to. He's had plenty of opportunity, and a certain amount of provocation.'

Temple shook his head. 'Anyhow, we'll soon find out one thing now.'

'What's that?'

'Whether Forbes is right about Sir Felix being The Marquis.'

They relapsed into silence, speculating on the possibilities of the idea. Over coffee, Steve noticed that Temple's thoughts were far away, so she glanced at the lunchtime edition of the evening paper which she had bought outside. In the 'Stop Press' there was a stereotyped report of Sir Felix's accident, which might well have been sent in by the local correspondent of the paper, and slightly amplified by a sub-editor with the help of *Who's Who*.

Steve read it through carefully, then laid the paper aside and allowed herself to recall some of her recent meetings with Sir Felix. She was interrupted by a suggestion from Temple that they should spend the afternoon witnessing the new Marx Brothers film which had just arrived in the West End.

An hour later, having successfully dozed through two Ministry of Information features, a couple of newsreels and a 'documentary' about Irish village life, Steve woke up and laughed immoderately at the antics of the Marx Brothers. Then the lights went up, and she looked round the dazed, rather vacuous faces of their fellow patrons. Suddenly Steve clutched Temple's sleeve.

'Paul, look at that man sitting by himself over there!'

Temple followed her direction.

'Well?'

'It's – it's that Sergeant Morris who called for me at The Silver Swan.'

Temple stared intently, and was about to rise to his feet when the lights went down again. He pulled out the small torch he always kept in an inside pocket, and made his way across the auditorium. But by the time he reached the other side, the man had vanished through one of the three exits on that side of the theatre.

Temple waited for Steve to join him in the foyer.

'Paul,' she said, anxiously, 'you don't think he's following us, do you?'

'I wish him joy if he is,' he replied grimly. 'Let's go back to the flat and get Pryce to toast large quantities of crumpets.'

Outside the cinema Temple hailed a taxi, and when they were inside, Steve could not restrain the impulse to peep through the back window to see if there was any sign of pursuit. But she found it almost impossible to detect any likely vehicle amongst the tremendous stream of traffic that was following.

After tea, Temple lay back in his armchair and discoursed at some length upon the plot of a new thriller novel that had been simmering in his brain for the past fortnight.

Steve looked at him admiringly.

'I really don't know how you do it,' she confessed. 'I'd have thought this Marquis case was worrying you to death, and taking up every minute of your time.'

'I'm only obeying the Chief Commissioner's advice to go home and write a novel,' he laughed. 'Anyhow, it's quite a tonic to escape from fact into fiction sometimes. And yet again, it's often salutary to go from fiction to cold, hard facts.'

'I never realised Sir Felix was sixty-nine,' said Steve suddenly, for no apparent reason.

'Didn't you?' replied Temple, indifferently. 'I always thought he looked quite seventy-two or three.'

Steve noticed that he did not seem particularly anxious to discuss Sir Felix, and indeed had made no reference to him all the afternoon. It was as if he were concentrating the full force of his reasoning powers upon some other line of attack.

'I don't think he should have driven a car at his age,' persisted Steve. 'If he could afford two large houses like that, he could surely have kept a chauffeur and—'

Temple yawned and stubbed out his cigarette.

'Darling, d'you happen to know if I have a presentable dress waistcoat? I'll probably be needing it this evening.'

'Of course darling. Two came back from the cleaners yesterday. I gave them to Pryce to put away. Shall I tell him ...?'

She half rose from her chair, but he waved her back.

'No, no, I'll do it.'

Temple went out into the hall, called Pryce and gave him instructions, then engaged in two brief telephone conversations, of which Steve caught only meaningless snatches.

'Paul,' she began, when he returned. 'Do you think that really was an accident?'

He took out his watch and compared it with the clock on the mantelpiece.

'Oh yes, it was an accident all right,' he replied, casually. 'I say, is that clock right?'

'Two minutes fast.'

'H'm, we haven't much time. How long will it take you to dress?'

'But I'd no idea I was going out with you,' she protested. 'I thought it was one of your Club dinners.'

'Of course you're coming with me – it's quite a social occasion,' he informed her. 'I just arranged it on the phone, and believe me, it's very special.'

'But Paul, what sort of place are we going to?'

'You might wear that powder blue frock,' he answered. 'It would be most suitable.'

'I daresay, Paul, but ...'

'And we haven't much time, darling. You'll have to hurry.'

Steve's protests were cut short by a ring at the outside bell, and Pryce ushered in Sir Graham Forbes.

When Pryce had departed the Commissioner told them that he had decided to visit Oxford Circus himself, and had in fact only just returned from there.

'Well, what happened?' asked Temple.

Forbes shrugged impatiently.

'Not a damn thing.'

'Did the Honourable Charles Serflane turn up?'

'Oh yes,' grunted Forbes, 'he was there all right, complete with suitcase! The poor devil looked as if he was in the middle of a nightmare! He waited almost an hour for the girl.'

'But she never arrived?'

'No,' said Forbes. 'Not as far as we know.' The Commissioner was obviously keyed up, and had difficulty in suppressing his excitement. 'And do you know what I think, Temple?' he cried excitedly. 'I think that proves without a shadow of doubt that Sir Felix Reybourn is The Marquis.'

As he spoke he suddenly turned and stood in a challenging attitude with his back to the fire.

Temple did not speak.

'Well, if Sir Felix was The Marquis, your troubles are over, Sir Graham,' said Steve lightly. 'And now if you'll excuse me, I must go and change.'

Forbes looked from Temple to Steve with ill-concealed curiosity.

'Er – are you two going somewhere?' he asked.

'We are,' replied Steve, 'but where exactly, I haven't the least idea.'

When they were alone Temple offered Forbes a cigarette and lit one himself.

'Sorry to have to run off, Sir Graham, but I know you'll understand. I'll have to go and get into my glad rags. No! No, don't run away. Help yourself to a drink!'

'Thanks,' murmured Forbes, splashing a generous quantity of whisky into a tumbler. 'I say, where are you two going, if it isn't a rude question?'

Temple turned at the door.

'You'd be surprised, Sir Graham,' he replied, with an amused smile. 'By Timothy, you'd be surprised!'

A few hours earlier that evening, Forbes was sitting in his car issuing last-minute instructions to the Honourable Charles Serflane. Charles Serflane was a thin, pale young man with hair that was almost white.

'The letter didn't say which entrance to the tube station,' said Serflane, rather plaintively. He had been screwing himself up for this ordeal since mid-day, and having drunk three brandies before he started out, was now experiencing a pleasant internal glow. He had in fact already begun to delude himself that he, Charles Serflane, was going to bring the redoubtable Marquis to book. Indeed, after a chequered career amidst the more dubious West End element, the Honourable Charles Serflane was at last about to make good!

He clutched his little attache case stuffed with old newspapers. Privately, he had decided to ignore Forbes' instructions, and as soon as the girl showed herself take charge of the situation. After all, the detectives might be too late, and miss their quarry in the crowd. Nothing like a bit of action on the spot, decided the Honourable Charles. After all, why should Scotland Yard claim all the credit, while he was thrust into the background as the mere receiver of the blackmailing letter?

'I should try the Oxford Street entrance first,' suggested Forbes, glancing at the clock on the dashboard. 'It's nearly half-past now. Better get going – and remember what I told you.'

Serflane nodded and slowly climbed out of the car. Amidst the surging crowds of Oxford Street, he did not feel so secure. The Marquis might be lurking in any of these doorways. He walked the fifty yards or so to the entrance of the tube station, and stood uncertainly regarding the stream of people rushing past him. He hoped the detectives were within easy reach, and on their toes.

He speculated as to what this girl would be like. Maybe he would recognise her. Probably he would have come across her in one of the many night clubs he had patronised during the past five years. In that case, he decided, he would most certainly follow up the case himself. Or would he? He recalled one or two of the shadier type of women he had encountered in an unpleasant frame of mind, and shuddered at the recollection.

A stout woman bumped into him and he caught his breath in fear. But she paid him no further attention and bustled off into the station below.

Ten minutes went by, and Serflane began to get restless. Out of the corner of his eye, he saw Forbes standing in the entrance to a large store opposite. The Honourable Charles suddenly felt very self-conscious, as he stood there, clasping his attache case. To the hundreds of people who surged past him, he was just a city clerk waiting for a girl to turn up, and getting a little more agitated as every minute passed. There were half-a-dozen detectives nearby expecting him to play his part. There was a strange woman expecting him to hand over that innocent case. How could he avoid looking rather strained?

Another thought struck him. Supposing the woman had already arrived. Suppose she were surveying him carefully from some point of vantage. The Honourable Charles fingered his tie uneasily and looked round as casually as possible. There were several women gazing in shop windows near at hand – it might be one of them, waiting to make quite certain that the coast was clear.

He felt that he could stand the strain no longer. He had to make a move of some sort. He walked down the steps and into the booking hall. Streams of people seemed to be perpetually swirling around him. He became tired of looking into women's faces for some sign of recognition. After a while, he strolled over to the bookstall and gazed with unseeing eyes at the array of books and periodicals. Hot gusts of air from the tube below swept past him as every train volleyed into the station. The homeward rush was slackening a little now. Serflane looked at his watch once more. Ten minutes to seven. He decided to walk up the stairs to the Regent Street exit, and he waited about five minutes. Still no one accosted him.

He began to wonder if this was some stupid joke of Laraine's. Of course, she had sworn she knew nothing about it, and that the letters had been stolen from her flat. Still, that was the sort of thing she would say if she had been planning some trickery of this sort. Serflane frowned thoughtfully as he speculated upon this possibility. He had been crazy about Laraine at one time, but this did not blind him to the fact that she was not over-scrupulous about other people's property or feelings. There was that time when the club was raided, and Laraine had picked up an exquisitely chased gold cigarette case which one of the guests had left behind in her hurried exit. Charles had told her that he had an idea the case belonged to Lady Welland, but Laraine had merely shrugged her pretty shoulders and made no attempt to pursue the matter.

Then there was that fur coat for which he had given her a cheque for nine hundred guineas. He had seen an identical mink coat in a shop in Bond Street marked £650. At that time, he had been too infatuated to inquire into the matter. But he had always wondered ...

He walked slowly and thoughtfully round the corner of Regent Street and back to the Oxford Street entrance of the tube station.

Meanwhile, Inspector Ross, who had followed him into the booking hall, had decided that he would be less conspicuous if he took up his position inside a telephone booth, and kept an eye on Serflane from there. After he had busied himself with the telephone directory, he picked up the receiver as if he were making a call, and pretended to be listening. In this manner he watched Serflane for quite five minutes, standing with his back to the right-hand side of the booth.

As Serflane went up the steps to the Regent Street exit, Ross replaced the receiver, and opened the door of the booth. Then he noticed that a woman was leaving the box on his left. He had been standing with his back to her, or he would have recognised her at once.

'Well!' he exclaimed. 'What brings you here?'

She gave him a cold stare.

'I just happen to be minding my own business,' she retorted, insolently. 'Pity some other people can't do the same.'

And with that Parthian shot, Dolly Fraser swept past Ross, pushed through the barrier, and vanished down the escalator.

Temple gave the taxi-driver the name of their destination in a discreet aside, and it was not until they had travelled some distance that Steve found an opportunity to interrupt her husband's light-hearted chatter and ask: 'Paul, where *are* we going?'

'Oh, just a night club, darling!'

'But we seem to have been travelling for hours.'

Steve peered through the window into the blackness, and she somehow got the impression that they were at the Northern end of Baker Street.

'Paul,' she cried in exasperation, 'if you don't tell me where we're going, I'll get out and walk.'

'Then I fail to see how you'd get there,' he replied, urbanely. 'I've already told you we're going to a night club.'

'Do I know it?'

'I should imagine not – though I never quite fathom the extent of your general knowledge. It's called The Clockwise.'

'I've never heard of it,' said Steve. 'Is it one of those draughty cellars where one pays ridiculous prices for food and drink?'

'One pays ridiculous prices, all right, but it is emphatically not a cellar. A couple of years ago it was called The Oriental, and before that The Madagascar. In those days it had a most peculiar reputation and was run by a man called Arnaud Perriolia. It was Perriolia who bought up the adjoining premises for extensions, and had lifts installed. In fact, he transformed it into a veritable Corner House of night clubs. Nowadays, of course, it's highly respectable, and shunned by all the gay young set accordingly. I remember going there one night just before I met you—'

'I believe you, darling,' interrupted Steve, urgently. 'But what are we going there for now?'

Temple lighted a cigarette quite deliberately.

'Because I have an appointment,' he replied, in a level tone. 'Rather an important one.'

'Would it be indiscreet to ask who with?'

Temple placed a foot on the opposite seat and smiled in the darkness.

'It's no use telling you, Steve. You simply wouldn't believe me.'

'Why not try me?' she suggested, in a voice which seemed to suggest that her patience was almost exhausted.

Temple expelled a mouthful of smoke.

'Very well,' he agreed, as one who is making a generous concession. 'I have an appointment with Sir Felix Reybourn.'

CHAPTER XIV

'The Clockwise'

STEVE was still bewildered and confused when the taxi wheezed to a standstill.

'Here we are,' said Temple, opening the door before the driver could get round, and stepping on to the pavement.

'But Paul, surely Sir Felix is ...'

'Now, no more questions, darling! Your friends might still be following us.'

He turned to pay the taxi-driver, and they made their way towards the dim blue light which was the only indication of the entrance to the club. Steve held his arm tightly, blinking as they came into the brilliant lights of the entrance lounge. Several people, all of them expensively dressed, were chatting desultorily while they waited for their friends. From the distance came the steady beat of drums and the gentle wail of the saxophone. The music grew louder as a glass-panelled door opened, and a middle-aged man of slightly swarthy appearance came to welcome Temple with outstretched arms.

'Hello Gus, how are you?' smiled the detective.

Gus began to rub his hands.

'I am fine, Mr. Temple, but this is the first time you have honoured us by bringing Mrs. Temple.'

'I promised I would. It's rather an important occasion.' Temple turned and introduced Steve.

Gus bowed.

'I am honoured, Mrs. Temple. The Clockwise is honoured!'

'All right, Gus,' interrupted Temple. 'My wife was once a reporter, so addresses of welcome don't mean a thing in her young life!' He handed over his hat and coat to the smiling cloakroom attendant.

'I think you will find everything has been arranged, Mr. Temple,' said Gus.

'Is Maisie here?'

Before Gus could answer, the panelled door swung open again to reveal a vivacious titian blonde of just under average height. She wore an emerald green chiffon dress, and her every line and movement exuded self-confidence.

'Hello Paul!' she cried in exuberant tones, flinging her arms around him with a complete disregard for any spectators. Temple gravely disentangled himself.

'Why Maisie! It's good to see you again!' he laughed.

'And I guess this is Mrs. Temple,' she hazarded, indicating Steve. 'I always used to warn you, Paul, that you'd fall for a dark-eyed charmer!'

'Steve, this is Maisie Delaway, an old friend of mine,' said Temple. Maisie took Steve's hand, and eyed her appraisingly.

'You certainly can pick 'em, brother,' she decided. 'Glad to know you, Mrs. Temple. I've heard a lot about you. Paul and I are old friends, you know.' She displayed a flash of teeth that would have done credit to a dental advertisement.

'Yes, I rather got that impression,' said Steve, just a little bewildered, and wondering what would happen next.

'We met way back in Chicago – or was it Kansas City? – in 1931,' continued Maisie in her attractive husky voice. 'Those were the days!'

'Oh,' said Steve, suddenly enlightened. 'You're *that* Maisie! Paul told me about you when we were in Chicago. But I thought he said your name was Maisie Kelvin?'

'So it was. I've changed it twice since then,' laughed Maisie. 'But my luck remains much about the same!'

'Paul always told me how lucky you were,' said Steve, recalling to mind some of the varied phases of Maisie's hectic career which Temple had related at odd times.

Starting life as a dancer in a juvenile troupe that clung precariously to the fifth-rate vaudeville circuits, Maisie had always been the star performer amongst the bunch of chattering precocious youngsters. This fact had not escaped her notice, and at the age of ten she threatened to resign and start her own solo act unless her salary was raised to eight dollars a week. The ex-ballet dancer who ran the troupe could cheerfully have murdered Maisie, but she had to give way, for she was well aware that most of her bookings depended upon the light comedy touches with which Maisie enlivened a singularly uninspired set of mechanical movements.

Maisie picked up new routines like a circus terrier acquires fresh tricks, and was showing every sign of developing into a first-rate comedienne when, at the age of twelve, appearing in a back-street burlesque theatre in Los Angeles, she succumbed to the lure of Hollywood. For six lonely, heart-breaking months, she trailed round the agents and studios, and at the end of the six months it dawned on Maisie that Hollywood had no use for her! So in desperation she joined a small-time family act, playing five shows a day, week in, week out, and wearing through a pair of dancing shoes every two months.

It was not surprising that by the time Maisie reached the age of eighteen, she looked twenty-five and was more experienced in the ways of the world than most women of forty. Prohibition came into force soon after her eighteenth birthday, and brought with it the inevitable army of bootleggers and their satellites. Among the latter was a certain Luke Zwar, with whom Maisie scraped up an acquaintance. Luke had ambition. He intended to join the bootlegger kings just as quickly as his nimble brain would propel him to the top of that strange profession. Incidentally, Luke prided himself on recognising a good thing when he saw it. He saw Maisie!

Before the war was out, 'Maisie's Craze' was on the way to being one of the most popular speakeasies in Chicago, and Maisie – who sang Sophie Tucker songs and acted as mistress of ceremonies – was widely recognised as a figure of some importance. The liquor at Maisie's Craze was, of course, supplied exclusively by Luke Zwar, at an average profit of a thousand dollars a week.

'Not bad for a start, kid,' Luke told her in their apartment one evening, 'but we're going to do this in a big way. Next month, we open a Maisie's Craze in Pittsburg and another in Toledo. Inside a year, I'll have a chain of 'em right across the States. Guess that'll keep you busy looking after the cabarets.'

But it turned out that Zwar was too ambitious, for, although he opened a dozen speakeasies, there was only one Maisie, and while the Chicago speakeasy showed increasing profits, these were eaten away by losses on others, where the territory was less favourable.

Matters were slowly beginning to improve, when Zwar was killed in a fracas with a rival gang who were trying to break in on his territory.

*

But Maisie's reputation as a night club queen was now established, and there was keen rivalry for her services. She decided to break away from Chicago and all its associations, and accepted an offer to open a new club at Kansas City, where Paul Temple had met her for the second time, being quite needlessly introduced by a friendly police official. They had renewed their strange friendship, this night club hostess and the young detective-novelist. They had sat up till four o'clock one morning while she told him the events of the two years since they had first met.

Although she had been in Kansas City less than a year, Maisie knew everybody with any 'pull,' and found a new interest in putting the Englishman, who had such a lively sense of humour, wise to local proceedings. Now in her twenties, she was beginning to penetrate a little deeper into various aspects of life outside her own rather artificial surroundings, and never tired of asking Temple questions on every subject under the sun. She was always a little awed at the fact that he was a Master of Arts, and actually made a living by writing books. Temple, on his side, was equally intrigued by the naive questions asked by this amazing young woman who had seen so much of the seamy side of life in such a short time.

She was very sorry when he had to return to New York, and she made him promise to visit her whenever he was in America. This had not always been possible, but he had managed to find her on two other occasions – once in Baltimore and then in New York, where her reputation as a cabaret star was second only to that of Dwight Fiske.

'Now remember, if ever you come to England, phone me as soon as you dock,' had been his parting injunction, and

Maisie had promised to do so. But she had forgotten her promise and had been established in London for quite a little while before, shortly after their return from America, Paul Temple realised that the ruling spirit at The Clockwise was none other than his old friend Maisie Delaway. When he did realise it Temple had no hesitation in asking her to help him out of a difficulty: a difficulty which he had explained to her in outline without going into detail.

'Well, how is the guest of honour?' he asked her, as she squeezed his arm affectionately.

'Oh, he's swell,' she replied, with a laugh. 'Queer old bird – we seem to talk different languages, but I guess we understand each other.'

'So you've been gossiping, eh?'

'Oh yes, I talk to him about dance routines and bootleggers, and he comes back about ancient Egypt. Never a dull moment, as you might say!'

She stopped her chattering for a second, looked at Temple curiously, and asked:

'Say, confidentially, Paul, what's the layout in this business?'

He brought his face near to hers and whispered.

'Confidentially, Maisie, it's confidential!'

Maisie shrugged her shapely white shoulders.

'I catch on! Well, you'll find him on the second floor, first door on the right.'

She pressed a button and the lift slid silently down to them. As soon as they were ascending, Steve turned to her husband.

'Maisie seems an even closer friend than I thought.'

'Practically a sister,' Temple assured her. 'And she's a friend in need all right this time.'

'But, seriously, Paul, is Sir Felix alive?'

'Very much so, as you'll see in a few moments.'

They found the door Maisie had mentioned, and on opening it, Steve was surprised to hear the voices of Sir Felix and Superintendent Bradley. She was even more surprised to see them sitting, in comfortable armchairs on either side of the electric fire, in a modernly furnished small lounge.

They rose to their feet and wished the bewildered Steve a polite 'good evening.' Sir Felix appeared quite at ease as he shook hands with her, and begged her to take his chair.

'Are you all right, Sir Felix? Quite comfortable here?' inquired Temple as they settled down.

Sir Felix offered a chocolate from a large box, then took one himself.

'Yes, I'm all right,' he replied. 'Providing I don't have to stay here too long.' He looked round the room, eyeing the lavishly inscribed signed portraits on the wall. 'I've been in some queer places in my time, but I'm getting a little old for these adventures.'

'I quite appreciate that, Sir Felix,' said Temple, seriously. 'I particularly asked Miss Delaway to see you have everything you want.'

'Oh Miss Delaway looks after me very well,' said Sir Felix. 'Indeed the young lady seems to be quite a character!' He chuckled reminiscently.

Bradley at last succeeded in cornering Temple, and, looking very worried, asked: 'Have you seen Sir Graham, Mr. Temple?'

'Now there's nothing for you to worry about, Bradley. I gave you my word on that, and I shan't let you down.'

'I know that, sir, but I am a bit worried. I'm not used to working on these lines, and if anything should go wrong ...'

'I quite appreciate your position, Bradley,' said Temple, patting his shoulder. 'And whatever happens, I'll take full responsibility.'

'Yes sir, I know you'll do what you can. But after all, you're outside the Yard, and it's against all our rules.'

'I'm afraid, Bradley, we've got to break rules with the same impunity as The Marquis if we're going to run him down.'

'But was all this necessary, Temple?' interposed Sir Felix. 'It seems rather a melodramatic precaution, if you don't mind my saying so.'

'I quite agree about its melodramatic possibilities,' said Temple, gravely, 'but I assure you, Sir Felix, it's highly essential just the same.'

'I wish to goodness someone would tell me what *has* happened!' cried Steve in bewilderment.

Temple offered his cigarette case to the others, then turned to Steve.

'I'll tell you what has happened, darling,' he began, in a soothing tone. 'A series of highly incriminating developments have indicated beyond any shadow of doubt that Sir Felix is The Marquis. Accordingly, Sir Graham issued a warrant for his arrest, and sent Bradley to execute the warrant. I knew this was bound to happen, however, and I told Bradley that under no circumstances was Sir Felix to be arrested.'

He tapped a cigarette on his case preparatory to lighting it, and coolly added: 'So the accident was faked.'

'But darling, you can't hope to get away with that,' cried Steve, in amazement.

'I don't hope to do so indefinitely. All I need is twenty-four hours' grace – possibly forty-eight hours. Quite a lot can happen in that time, Steve. Revolutions have been successfully staged in less.' He lit his cigarette, expelled two neat smoke rings, and repeated, 'Yes, a lot can happen in forty-eight hours.'

'I hope so, Mr. Temple,' declared Bradley, fervently, 'I sincerely hope so!'

CHAPTER XV

Above Suspicion

ON reaching the office the following morning, Sir Graham was surprised to hear that Temple had been awaiting his pleasure since nine o'clock. Eventually, he found him in the Records Department busily comparing specimens of handwriting with the help of a magnifying glass, and carrying on a desultory conversation with a young sergeant at the same time.

'Good morning, Sir Graham,' said Temple, briskly, pushing a small pile of cards into a corner, and returning the lens to its owner.

'Hello, Temple,' said Forbes, gruffly. 'You're an early bird, aren't you?'

'Well, I daresay you've heard the legend about the early bird,' smiled Temple.

'H'm,' murmured Forbes sceptically.

'Quite an unfounded legend of course,' pursued Temple, pleasantly, 'I daresay you've noticed that the more money men make, the later they seem to arrive at the office. And I don't suppose even you know the reason why, Sir Graham.'

'No,' grunted Forbes, taking a paper from under his arm and unfolding it. 'There's a lot of questions I'd like answered. Have you seen the *Morning Express?*'

'I'm afraid getting up so early was such an effort, Sir Graham, that I haven't had time to look at a paper.'

'H'm, then take a look at this ...'

He pointed to a two-inch headline splashed across the back page.

MYSTERY OF SIR FELIX REYBOURN BELIEVED TO BE
ALIVE – ANOTHER SCOTLAND YARD MYSTERY

Temple skimmed through the heavy type summary of the story.

'H'm, it certainly sounds like a scoop for somebody,' he murmured, in non-committal tones.

'But it's a lot of damned nonsense. Not a word of truth in it!' snapped Sir Graham. 'Why, Bradley identified the body, and I've never known him to slip up on any case.'

'I'll 'phone Castleton, the news editor, if you like; he's quite a friend of mine,' Temple offered. 'I'm interested to hear how they got hold of that story.'

'These damned editors never let on,' snapped Forbes. 'I've tried it myself.'

'I think I can fix it with Castleton,' said Temple. 'We're old friends, and he knows I respect anything he tells me in confidence. What's more, I've given him a scoop or two in my time.'

'H'm, well, there's no harm in trying. You can 'phone him from my office. I'll be with you in ten minutes – one or two things I may as well check while I'm down here ...'

When he got back to his office, Sir Graham found Temple carefully re-reading the report, which was phrased in the slick style of the modern newspaper reporter, adding just the right amount of imagination to the few facts at the writer's disposal.

'Well, any luck?' asked Forbes.

Temple laid down the paper.

'In a way,' he replied. 'Castleton was highly delighted I'd rung up, because there's apparently some mystery about that report. One of the night "subs" found it on his desk after he'd been having a snack in the canteen. It was just in time for the final edition, written in typescript, and it was signed with the initials of one of their most reliable reporters, the chief "sub" O.K.'d it right away.'

'And who was the reporter?'

'A fellow called Jimmy Fane.'

'Oh yes, I know Fane quite well,' said Forbes.

'Apparently, the trouble is Fane knows nothing about this report,' continued Temple. 'He's on the daytime shift this week, and last night enjoyed a convivial evening at the Cheshire Cheese. Doesn't remember an awful lot about it. When he rolled into the office about 8.30 this morning, Castleton sent for him to do a follow-up on the Reybourn story – only to find that Jimmy hadn't the remotest idea what it was all about.'

Forbes snorted.

'So it's all a confounded hoax! Why the devil didn't they telephone us for a check-up before they put the report in? Now I suppose we'll get the Home Office screaming blue murder again,' he added, grimly.

'You can always tell them the old one about the freedom of the press,' grinned Temple. Forbes sat down at his desk and began to look through his letters. 'Oh well, we may as well forget all about it and get on with the job,' he growled.

'Not so fast, Sir Graham,' said Temple, perching on the corner of the desk. 'It's obviously to the interest of someone to take all that trouble and risk to get the story in the *Morning Express.*'

'You mean The Marquis?'

'Who else?'

'But why should he?'

'Surely that's fairly obvious, Sir Graham. The man we're after has succeeded in throwing a considerable amount of suspicion upon Sir Felix Reybourn. Naturally, if he is going to continue with his nefarious activities, it's to his advantage to keep on throwing suspicion on to Sir Felix by suggesting that he isn't dead at all, and is still operating from some place of concealment.'

'Might be something in that,' conceded the Chief Commissioner. 'But it doesn't seem to get us very far.'

Temple smiled. 'But it does explain the mystery of the report in the *Morning Express.*' He picked up the paper again, the door opened, and Ross appeared.

'I'm sorry, sir,' Ross apologised. 'I didn't know you were engaged.'

'That's all right, Inspector. What is it?'

'It's only my rough draft of the report on the Pevensey affair – I thought you might like to see it before I send it down to be typed.'

'Good,' said Sir Graham, pushing aside his correspondence, 'I'll just glance through it.' He took the neatly written sheets, and while he was turning them over, Ross glanced across at Temple.

'Anything interesting in the paper, Mr. Temple?'

'Then you haven't seen the *Morning Express,*' replied Temple, passing it over.

'No sir, not this morning.'

'Apparently, they have a hunch that Reybourn is still alive,' said Temple drily, indicating the report in question.

Ross read the headlines and gave vent to a low whistle.

'But this is all nonsense, Mr. Temple,' he protested. 'Why, Bradley identified the body, and he's never been known to make a mistake of that sort.'

Temple nodded.

'All the same,' he insisted quietly, 'it would be rather good news if Reybourn were not dead, wouldn't it, Inspector?'

'Yes,' reflected Ross. 'Yes, indeed it would, Mr. Temple.'

Forbes glanced up from his papers.

'You'd better leave this report with me, Ross. Just one or two little things I want to look into. I'll send it down to you sometime before lunch.'

'Very good, sir.'

Ross discreetly withdrew.

Deep in thought, Temple crossed to the large bay window. He stood for a moment looking down into the square below. At last he said: 'Sir Graham, do you remember that envelope we found on Roddy Carson? The one with Sir Felix Reybourn's address on it?'

Forbes looked up quickly.

'Why yes, I've got it here!'

He opened a drawer and took out a handful of his coloured folders. At length, he came across the somewhat grimy envelope.

'I always had a profound admiration for your system, Sir Graham,' declared Temple solemnly, with the merest suggestion of a twinkle in his eye.

'Well, what about this envelope?' insisted Forbes, calmly ignoring the compliment.

But Temple was not to be hurried.

'Now, Sir Graham, you remember the letter Storey brought us, the one from The Marquis to the Hon. Charles Serflane?'

'Yes, I remember it. We checked up on the handwriting – it's the same as that on this envelope.'

'That's very interesting,' Temple murmured, pensively.

'What are you getting at, Temple?' asked Forbes, suspiciously.

'Just this, Sir Graham. I was wondering if you would care to compare the writing on the envelope with that on the report in front of you.'

'But—but this is Inspector Ross's report,' stuttered Forbes, incredulously.

'Compare them, Sir Graham,' insisted Temple in the gentle tone one reserves for a fractious child. Forbes blinked, then looked at the report. The red second finger of the electric wall clock swept nearly full circle before the Chief Commissioner spoke again.

'Good God! It isn't possible!'

'They're the same writing?' queried Temple, diffidently.

'Exactly!' Forbes was completely staggered. 'Temple! What the devil does this mean?'

'I'll tell you what it means, Sir Graham,' said Temple, very deliberately.

He crossed the room and carefully closed the door which Inspector Ross had left slightly ajar.

While Temple was in his bath that evening, Roger Storey was announced, and Steve received him in the lounge. Storey had now discarded his sling, and he seemed to have more colour in his cheeks than Steve remembered noticing before.

'Mr. Temple said he wanted to see me rather particularly,' he told Steve. 'But if it isn't convenient I can easily call back later.'

'No, no, do sit down, Mr. Storey,' she urged. 'I'm sure Paul won't be more than a few minutes. Can I get you a drink of any sort?'

He shook his head. 'No thanks. I know it sounds a trifle heroic, but I'm on the waggon just for a time.' He smiled somewhat deprecatingly.

'Well come to the fire,' Steve invited. 'Here's the evening paper. I'll just go and hurry Paul if you'll excuse me.'

Storey thrust his feet towards the blaze and opened the paper.

Temple entered the room a few minutes later wearing a dressing-gown that would have done credit to the most hectic Noel Coward comedy.

Roger Storey looked up from his paper, then jumped up.

'Good evening, Mr. Temple. I got your telephone message – sorry I was out when you rang.'

Temple noticed that he wore another new suit.

'That's all right,' said Temple. 'Excuse this exotic dressing-gown. It's my wife's idea of what the popular novelist should wear! Actually, I've never been to China!'

Roger laughed, then once again refused a drink. Temple mixed himself a small whisky and soda, which he brought over to the fire.

He looked thoughtfully into the fire for a few moments before he spoke.

'I asked you to drop in for a chat,' he began, 'because – well, the fact of the matter is, I want you to do me a favour.'

'Why certainly,' replied Roger eagerly, his eyes alight with interest.

Temple sipped his whisky; he appeared to be in some doubt as to how to broach the subject he had in mind.

'I think,' he said slowly, 'you know Inspector Ross, by sight at any rate.'

Roger seemed slightly surprised.

'Yes, of course I know Ross,' he replied.

Temple appeared to be about to reveal some information, then paused and asked: 'What do you think of him?'

'Oh – er – he seems a pleasant sort of chap,' answered Roger, rather at a loss. 'Why do you ask?'

Temple tasted his whisky and soda.

'Storey,' he said quietly, 'I want you to trail Ross.'

There was a moment's pause before Temple continued:

'I want you to make a daily report to me of everywhere Ross goes. I want to know everything he does! The people he meets! Will you do that for me?'

'Trail a police inspector?' echoed Storey, in bewildered tones.

'That's what I said.'

Storey looked away in some embarrassment.

'But surely Ross is above suspicion,' he protested.

'No one is above suspicion, Storey,' said Temple, eyeing him over his glass. 'Not even you, or Ross, or Bradley, or Mrs. Clarence—or even Sir Graham if it comes to that. We have to suspect everybody.'

'You're quite sure about this?' asked Roger after a moment's hesitation.

'I'd hardly have asked you to come here if I weren't.'

Storey seemed to be weighing up the position.

'All right,' he decided at last. 'I'll do it, Temple!'

'I'm sure I can rely on you,' said Temple, gravely. 'Particularly after the experience you've had during the past few months.'

'I'm ready to tackle anything that'll bring to book the swine who killed Alice,' said Roger with sudden force. 'Do you know where Ross lives?'

Temple took a notebook off the shelf and read out: 'Forty-nine Birchfield Avenue, Wimbledon.'

Storey borrowed a pencil to scribble down the address on a slip of paper. Then he asked: 'When do you want me to start?'

'Tonight if possible. The sooner you can get on the job, the better. Something might break at any minute.'

'All right,' Roger agreed. 'I'll 'phone you tomorrow morning, about ten.'

He fastened his camel hair coat, picked up his hat, and moved slowly towards the door. As he opened it, he turned.

'All the same, Temple,' he murmured, shaking his head, 'it does seem a bit steep!'

Temple seemed particularly cheerful at breakfast next morning, rather to Steve's mystification, for he had told her very little about any later developments concerning The Marquis. Even a batch of singularly unenthusiastic press cuttings concerning his latest novel did not appear to depress him very much.

'I see the *Morning Express* is quite conceited about the Reybourn scoop,' she commented, tossing him the paper.

'H'm, they might have landed themselves in serious trouble, printing that story without official verification. As it happens to have come off, they're all cock-a-hoop. I'm surprised at Castleton, I thought he was a little more restrained.'

'That's life in Fleet Street,' murmured Steve. '"Dog eat dog." I suppose you broke the news to Sir Graham about Sir Felix when you were with him yesterday afternoon.'

'As there was an *Express* reporter waiting on the mat, I felt something had to be done.'

'What did he say?'

Temple grinned at the recollection. 'I regret to admit that he used some rather strong language, hardly consistent with his dignity as Chief Commissioner. Still, it passed off quite well, everything considered. Have you done with the marmalade, darling?'

'Poor Sir Graham,' Steve sympathised. 'You know, darling, if you have one really predominant fault, it's your malicious delight in keeping people in the dark. At this moment, I can't for the life of me make even a wild guess about what you're up to.'

He laughed. 'Well, that's something anyway, Steve!'

'Yes, but why pretend that Sir Felix is dead?' she insisted. Temple laid down the paper and began to spread marmalade on his toast.

'Simply because I wanted to know whether Sir Felix was The Marquis or not.'

'But I thought you'd already decided that he wasn't The Marquis,' she said in surprise.

'Did you, darling?' he replied glibly, avoiding her direct gaze.

'Look here, Paul,' she declared in some exasperation, 'It's no use your being mysterious with me—'

'Because you know all the answers, eh darling?' he laughed.

'Most of them, anyway,' she retorted, feeling a little cheated all the same. Her delight in discovering that Sir Felix was alive after all was now mingled with intense curiosity concerning his strange hideout. However, the appearance of Pryce forestalled any further cross-questioning.

'I beg your pardon, madam,' gently interrupted the butler, 'but Sir Graham Forbes would like to see Mr. Temple at once, if possible.'

'Ask him to come in here, will you, Pryce?'

Forbes was full of apologies: 'I didn't realise you'd be at breakfast, Temple.'

'This is one of the mornings when I do not perform my early bird act,' smiled Temple. 'Sit down and have some coffee.'

'Thanks.'

Sir Graham drew off his gloves, and unbuttoned his overcoat.

'Try one of those cigarettes on the table; they're a new brand of Egyptian.'

Forbes hesitated, then took one. 'I don't usually smoke this early, but I can never resist trying a new brand.' He lighted the cigarette, and balanced a cup of black coffee on his knee. Almost at once, he laid the cigarette down, then took a sip at the coffee and placed the cup on the arm of his chair.

'Temple, you remember the letter that was sent to the Honourable Charles Serflane,' he began.

Temple took a bite at his toast and nodded.

'Apparently,' announced Forbes, 'he's received another.'

'How do you know?'

'Serflane was waiting for me when I got to the Yard this morning. He was with Bradley – they'd already checked up for fingerprints without any results. It seems the note arrived late last night by hand.'

He took the flimsy slip of pale blue notepaper from his pocket and passed it over to Temple, who read it through twice, then appeared to be lost in thought. Forbes picked up his cigarette again.

'Well, what d'you think of it, Temple?' he asked, at length.

Temple refolded the letter.

'I think,' he replied, deliberately, 'that this time, Sir Graham, he certainly means business.'

'Don't you think he meant business last time?' queried Forbes, with a lift of the eyebrows.

'No,' replied Temple, shortly.

'What makes you say that?'

'Well, no one turned up at the station,' Temple reminded him.

Forbes flicked the ash off his cigarette.

'For the simple reason that The Marquis found out that Serflane had taken the letter to Roger Storey, and that Storey had brought it to me.'

'What does this last letter say, darling?' Steve was anxious to know. Temple handed it to her, and she read:

Dear Sir,
This must be taken more seriously than the first note
I sent you, and moreover must be considered strictly
confidential. The letters written by you to Miss
Laraine Curtis are still in my possession. They are
still, in my humble opinion, worth precisely £7,000.
I suggest, therefore, that having secured this amount,
you meet me personally tomorrow evening, shortly
after eight o'clock in the lounge of the October
Hotel, Dalton Street, Kensington.

The Marquis.

Steve wrinkled her forehead, thoughtfully.

'Surely, he won't be there in person,' she was saying, trying to figure out the problem. A queer, strangled gasp from Sir Graham distracted her.

'Sir Graham, what's wrong?'

Forbes clutched at his collar, for a moment it seemed almost as if he was speechless. With a shaky hand, he pointed to the cigarette, which had fallen to the floor. Temple loosened the Chief Commissioner's collar while Steve ran for some brandy.

After a moment Paul Temple picked up the cigarette. It smelt exactly as one would expect an Egyptian cigarette to smell when burning.

Steve came running with the brandy, and Forbes took one or two sips with difficulty; it seemed to revive him for, in spite of Temple's attempt to restrain him, he struggled to his feet.

'Look out, he's going to fall!' cried Steve. Sir Graham swayed uncertainly, then seemed to lose consciousness completely.

As he pitched forward, the telephone began to ring insistently, until the air seemed to vibrate with its shrill message.

CHAPTER XVI

Superintendent Bradley
Goes To The Pictures

IT was Superintendent Bradley's afternoon off, but he was not particularly elated at the prospect. In fact, Bradley was in a singularly irascible frame of mind. For one thing, he was not at all happy about the Reybourn deception, having a vague idea that it would go down in his dossier as a very dubious sort of experiment. Forbes had not so far made much comment upon the episode, but Bradley knew that he did not approve of the faked accident. In all fairness he had to admit that he would not himself have been particularly enthusiastic if the positions had been reversed. It wasn't as if this move of Temple's had so far shown any results. Indeed Bradley began to have his doubts as to whether it would, but Forbes had apparently suspended judgment for the time being.

To upset Bradley's temper still further, relations between himself and Ross had been distinctly strained for the past few days, since Ross had been detailed to bring in Lannie Dukes. Bradley had greeted him every morning with an inquiry as to whether he had been successful. For Bradley rather fancied the idea of making some investigations himself in this direction, arguing that Dukes was known to have transmitted orders from The Marquis, and would therefore be quite likely to be in a position to reveal the identity of the leader of the organisation.

'Any news of Lannie?' asked Bradley, as Ross came into the office.

'No, I haven't any news!' snapped Ross. 'I've hung around all his pubs and hideouts till I'm just about sick of it.'

'Sure you haven't missed him?' queried Bradley.

There was a dangerous look in Ross's eyes.

'And why should I miss him?' he demanded, ominously.

'Well – er – he might be disguised,' suggested Bradley.

Ross was on the verge of losing his temper.

'Look here, Bradley, I haven't been at this game all these years without learning to see through any disguise,' he retorted. 'And if you're so damned anxious to pull him in, why don't you go after him yourself?'

The inter-office telephone buzzed and cheated Bradley of any reply. But it is extremely doubtful if he could have risen to the occasion.

Bradley and Ross hardly spoke to each other again that morning, and when Bradley caught a bus at one o'clock, he was still gloomily chewing the cud of his discontent, and vowing that he would somehow demonstrate that the task of bringing in Lannie Dukes was by no means beyond the powers of any normally endowed Scotland Yard official. The only trouble was he didn't quite know how to go about it. Lannie had disappeared from his haunts and was obviously playing for safety by losing himself in the metropolitan millions. Of course, Bradley could have sent out his description on the 'tape' to all stations, but that would be tantamount to admitting defeat. For several reasons, Bradley wanted the search kept as quiet as possible. He had a strong suspicion that The Marquis might get to know about it if Dukes' description was circularised. Also, he wanted to retain as much credit for himself as possible just in case the Reybourn 'accident' went on the debit side of his account. But Bradley was still inclined to be pessimistic as to the ways and means of tracking down the elusive Lannie Dukes.

When he arrived at the trim modern villa just off Denmark Hill, Bradley was still engaged in wracking his brain for some possible clue which would put him on the scent. As he opened the front gate, he heard the unmistakable shrill voice of seven-year-old April Bradley, and even as he inserted his latchkey in the front door she came running along the hall with the inevitable question:

'What have you brought me, Daddy?'

True, it happened to be April's birthday, but the question was so familiar, that Bradley had come to ignore it, and even on this momentous occasion had to admit that, under the stress of his working morning, he had completely forgotten his wife's whispered reminder as he left the house.

April showed her displeasure in the usual way, by sitting in the middle of the kitchen floor and screaming until she was red in the face. She was only pacified by a promise from Mrs. Bradley that Daddy would take her to the pictures that very afternoon. Bradley was about to expostulate, but interposed a grim, threatening glance from his wife, and subsided. He knew it was a waste of time to argue.

Though she was only five feet three and a half, and weighed just eight stone, Mrs. Bradley was in the habit of getting her own way with her husband. She had a ready tongue which was incisive without being unduly acidulous, and her steady brown eyes had a penetrating quality which her husband found some difficulty in withstanding. It was she who had insisted upon calling their only child April, and Bradley had agreed without demur, though he secretly considered it an affected name, and never used it, without feeling painfully self-conscious.

Under her mother's dominating influence, April had quickly developed into that despised abomination – a spoilt child. She was forever informing all and sundry that she was a little princess, and never stopped giving orders to the few occasional playmates who would put up with her overbearing ways. Yet April never failed to create a good impression on strangers, with her aureole of flaxen hair, deep brown eyes and perfectly shaped mouth.

Superintendent Bradley had little idea of the calculating thoughts that revolved around that shrewd mind; he was usually too immersed in some case or other to realise how gifts and favours were cunningly extorted from him as craftily as a con man lures on his victim.

As he ate his lunch, April chattered merrily of the films they would see, and what her beloved daddy would buy her in the shops; undismayed by his lack of response, she launched into a detailed account of a large doll she had seen the previous day.

'You're quiet,' commented Mrs. Bradley, a little affronted by the lack of co-operation her offspring was encountering.

'H'm,' grunted her husband, with his mouth full.

'Why can't you be pleasant to the child on her birthday?' demanded Mrs. Bradley.

'Taking her out, aren't I?' he demanded, truculently, for he did not greatly enjoy these excursions with the predatory April. And he had rather looked forward to spending this afternoon walking as far as Dulwich Park and reviewing the

Marquis case in his mind without the constant interruptions which April could be relied upon to provide. But he felt he had a duty to his daughter, and since he was fond of her in some ways, he would not have dreamed of trying to evade the special birthday treat.

After lunch, he lounged in an armchair while his wife busied herself transforming the incorrigible April into a dainty angelic cherub, all curls, blue bows and superficial innocence. It was difficult to tell whether mother or daughter was more pleased by the result of these labours.

With April clutching his hand determinedly, Bradley hailed a Number 68 bus, and hoisted his precious charge aboard, hardly noticing the middle-aged ladies who bestowed affectionate glances on the child and whispered approving comments to each other. But April missed none of them, and sat up straight on her seat with the gracious air of a sovereign on her throne, continuing to prattle of the doll she had seen, and which she was quite determined her Daddy should buy her before the day was out. Having been informed by his wife that the doll cost four pounds five shillings, Bradley was equally determined that he would put his foot down for once.

They got off the bus at Camberwell Green and began a tour of the cinemas. Bradley was rather attracted by one which was showing a re-issue of *Trader Horn*, but April was quite emphatic that this would not interest her. She finally led him down a back street to a cinema of which he had been previously ignorant, but which she had twice visited with her school friends. According to the lurid lithographs in front of the building, the current attraction was a breath-taking epic called *The Devil Riders*, and this apparently met with April's lavish approval.

Bradley asked for two balcony seats at the dingy box-office. They climbed the grimy staircase with its threadbare carpet, and entered the musty-smelling auditorium to be greeted with a sudden yell as a hundred lusty young throats cheered the progress of a man on horseback who was careering across the screen as if his very life depended on it.

In a penetrating voice, April ordered her father to buy her some chocolate from an attendant, then dragged him after her to a seat in the front row, squeezing past half-a-dozen grumbling patrons in the manner of an ancient queen spurning her slaves. She took charge of the chocolates as a matter of course, offering one to her obliging parent as an afterthought. They settled down to witness the exploits of the notorious Devil Riders, which at least served the purpose of reducing April to silence for as much as five minutes at a time, and which permitted Bradley to brood upon his own problems. The continuous din created by the younger section of the audience, however, grew to a positive uproar when the main feature ended, and was followed by a real old-fashioned serial, *The Killer Strikes Again*.

Bradley followed the lurid adventures of the intrepid Killer with a detached air, but April seemed to derive a considerable amount of entertainment from them.

It was getting dusk when they came out of the stuffy little cinema and walked back into the main thoroughfare, where April's attention was immediately attracted by the music and bright lights of an amusement arcade, into which she dragged her unwilling parent. Her mother had forbidden her to enter the place, but she knew that her father was not aware of that, and April was already versed in the insidious art of playing one parent against another for her own benefit.

171

The arcade was fairly full, chiefly of youths trying their luck at pin tables and other mechanical games of chance designed to induce the semi-educated to part with their hard-earned money. April made straight for a large glass case piled high with sweets and small toys, which were obligingly scooped up by a miniature crane and deposited in the waiting hand of anyone who cared to venture a penny. That most of its contents slid out of the scoop before they reached the speculator did not seem to deter the juvenile gamblers.

Bradley gave his progeny fourpence in coppers, and moodily looked round the place while she enjoyed herself. He wondered when the law would be adjusted to curtail the activities of such places. He looked along the arcade to the far end, where two or three youths were anxiously aiming air rifles at a number of objects which moved across the back of the stall.

'Come along gents – step this way and get your eye in ready for the invasion!' a hoarse voice was barking at intervals. For the first time, Bradley thought he recognised a familiar note in that voice. He looked inquiringly at the owner, then blinked as if unable to believe his eyes. But there could be no doubt about it. The flashily dressed, foxy-faced manager of the rifle range was Lannie Dukes.

Bradley stood quite still for some seconds, considering the best course of action. Then a small hand gripped his.

'More pennies, Daddy,' ordered Miss Bradley, cramming two very doubtful-looking confections into her mouth at once.

Bradley mechanically handed her twopence, and watched her spend it. Then he managed to persuade her to accompany him to the door.

'I want you to be a good girl and go straight home by yourself in a motor car, April,' said Bradley. But April seemed

172

to think the show should go on a little longer; the prospect of home and bed was not particularly exciting.

'Now, look here, April,' continued Bradley in some desperation, 'you go home now and I'll buy you that doll.'

'Tomorrow?' insisted the inexorable April.

Bradley agreed and April was satisfied. She knew a promise from her father was a sure guarantee. He took her a little way along the street to a taxi rank, gave a driver his address, deposited April inside the cab, scribbled a brief note to his wife on an old envelope, and April drove off, imagining herself in the inevitable role of princess conducting a triumphant procession through a loyal city.

Bradley returned to the amusement arcade and began slowly pushing his way to the far end. He was within ten yards of Dukes when the latter recognised him, broke off in the middle of his spiel, and abruptly turned and moved towards a door at the back of the range. Bradley lost no time in following him, and was just in time to see him turn into a room at the end of a short corridor. Bradley made a dive for the door, and was lucky enough to reach it just before Lannie could slam the door. The Superintendent burst into the room in time to see Lannie wrestling with a second door, which was obviously an emergency exit from the building.

Bradley caught him just as he had succeeded in wrenching open the door.

''Ere, you lemme go – you got nothing on me!' declared Lannie hoarsely, as he struggled to shake off Bradley's expert grip.

Bradley flung him into a chair and stood over him in a threatening attitude.

'We've got plenty on you, Lannie, and you know it! You were mixed up in the Bombay Road affair and you were one of the men who abducted Mrs. Temple! Oh yes, we've got plenty on you, Lannie. And it looks as if you'll get a longer stretch this time than all your others put together – unless you talk,' he added in a significant tone.

'You'll get nothing out of me.'

'Then you look like taking a holiday for about five years, maybe more when we prove you're definitely connected with The Marquis murders.'

'I tell you I ain't—'

'All right,' said Bradley curtly, 'it'll be the worse for you when we get definite proof. And I might tell you, Lannie, it's only a question of a day or two before Mr. Temple settles this business.'

The mention of Temple's name seemed to have more effect on Lannie than any of the previous threats. He licked his lips in nervous agitation, shuffled uncomfortably in his chair, looked round for some likely means of escape, but did not appear to find any.

'If I talk,' he suggested, ''ow do I know you'll let me get off light?'

Bradley shrugged. 'You've only got my word for it. But there's trouble coming to you in any case, Lannie, so I reckon you might as well take a chance.'

Lannie looked round the room again, as if he was afraid of being overheard.

'What d'yer want to know?' he demanded in a voice that was almost a whisper.

'Who sent you to pick up Mrs. Temple?' asked Bradley swiftly.

Lannie licked his lips again, and hesitated before murmuring: 'That was The Marquis.'

*

'And the Bombay Road place – was he running that?'

Lannie nodded. 'I just did what 'e told me – we all worked that way: 'e give us our orders every two days – told us where to pick up the stuff and where to drop it. He was never there more than ten minutes – we 'ardly set eyes on 'im.'

'Then who killed the Cartwright girl?'

'That was The Marquis.'

Lannie wiped the beads of perspiration from his forehead with the back of his hand.

'And I suppose it was The Marquis who gave you the tip that we were looking for you, and told you to lie low?' queried Bradley, thoughtfully.

Lannie nodded, but did not speak.

Bradley paused before going on. 'There's only one more question I want to ask you, Lannie.'

'Yes, sir, I think I know …'

'You've seen The Marquis? You could recognise him? You know who he really is?'

'Yes,' replied Lannie slowly. 'I know 'im all right, and you wouldn't ever guess who 'e was—not in a hundred years.'

Once more, he looked round anxiously, and then whispered: 'The Marquis is called …'

But before he could finish his sentence, the lights had snapped out; there was the muffled report of a silenced revolver, and Bradley felt Dukes' body crumple beneath his grasp. A door slammed. Bradley fumbled for the small torch he always carried and ran to the nearest door. He thought he heard footsteps along the corridor, then there was silence except for the raucous cacophony of the loudspeakers in the arcade.

CHAPTER XVII

Concerning Inspector Ross

THE telephone went on ringing for quite two minutes, while Steve and Temple struggled to lift Sir Graham into an armchair. They discovered that moving an inert body of some fourteen stone calls for a certain amount of expert knowledge and not a little brute strength. Finally, Temple placed his hands under Forbes' armpits, told Steve to grasp his feet, and with a concerted effort they managed to heave him into the chair.

After a moment Steve went across to the telephone and lifted the receiver.

'Hello? Oh, just a minute, Mr. Storey!'

She placed a hand over the mouthpiece.

'Ask him to meet me here at twelve-thirty,' Temple called to her. Steve gave the message, while Temple picked up Sir Graham's cigarette again, and once more studied it suspiciously. The cigarette had gone out now, and Temple detected a faint odour that was familiar. He went and poured out a cup of strong black coffee, which he brought back to the Chief Commissioner, who sighed and showed some signs of returning to consciousness.

'You must drink this, Sir Graham,' he urged. Forbes stirred slightly as the hot cup touched his lips. In small sips, he slowly swallowed about half its contents. Then he took a deep breath, sat up and looked round.

'I'm all right now,' he announced presently, and Temple noted that he was breathing more easily and that his normal ruddy colour had returned. 'That was a nasty turn, I wonder how—' he was beginning, but Temple interrupted.

'Better finish this coffee,' he advised. Forbes drained the cup, while his hosts watched him anxiously. At last, he set down the cup and saucer, and began to fasten his collar which Temple had loosened.

'I couldn't get my breath,' he told them. 'It was a most extraordinary sensation, worse than ordinary choking.' He felt the muscles of his throat in a tentative manner.

'You'll be all right in a few minutes,' Temple assured him.

'Yes, but what the devil was it, Temple?' persisted the Chief Commissioner.

'As you diagnosed before you went unconscious, Sir Graham, it was the cigarette.' Temple picked it up and handed it to him. Forbes sniffed it, wrinkled his forehead, but seemed very little the wiser.

'Where did you get them, Temple?'

'From my usual tobacconist in Regent Street.'

'But dammit man, we'd better 'phone him! If all this new brand is poisoned ...'

'Calm yourself, Sir Graham. They aren't. That particular cigarette was poisoned for the very special benefit of Steve or myself.'

'But who the devil would do that?' demanded Forbes in some mystification.

Temple smiled enigmatically. He found a small tin, and placed the cigarette inside it.

'I can think of one or two people who imagine they owe me a slight grudge,' he murmured. 'All the same, it was lucky you were drinking coffee, Sir Graham. The drug in the cigarette is rather a rare one. It's called Lokai – I believe its history goes right back to ancient days in Egypt.'

'Egypt?' repeated Forbes, sharply.

'No, no, Sir Graham, don't start that tack again. I can assure you that Sir Felix Reybourn hasn't been near this place since I bought the cigarettes.'

'Humph – you aren't obliged to see everyone who sneaks in while you're out!' retorted Sir Graham. 'But why was I lucky to be drinking coffee?'

'Because, strangely enough, black coffee is about the only antidote to Lokai,' Temple explained.

'In that case,' said Sir Graham, somewhat hastily, 'if it's all the same to you, I'll have another cup – just to make quite sure.' He passed his cup to Steve, who refilled it.

'Did Storey say he'd be here at half-past twelve?' asked Temple, also deciding to have another cup of coffee.

'Yes,' replied Steve. 'He seemed as cheerful as usual.'

Forbes looked across at Temple.

'Did you make those arrangements with Storey that you mentioned yesterday?' he asked.

'Yes, just as we agreed, Sir Graham,' replied Temple, diplomatically.

Forbes shook his head dubiously.

'Well, Ross isn't a fool, Temple. He's done some pretty smart work for the Special Branch at one time and another. It won't take him long to realise that Storey's trailing him.' He narrowed his eyebrows in perplexity. 'I can't think why you had to pick on an amateur like Storey. If you wanted Ross trailed, I've half-a-dozen first-class men right to hand ...'

'It's all right, Sir Graham,' said Temple, calmly. 'There's such a thing as killing two birds with one stone.'

Forbes shrugged. 'Well, it's your idea, and I hope it works. At least it gets Storey from under our feet for a while.'

'Poor Mr. Storey,' said Steve. 'He tries so hard, and I'm sure he means well.'

'Pity he hasn't a regular job to keep his mind occupied,' snorted Sir Graham, who was getting a little tired of Storey's persistent methods. 'What chance has he got against an experienced man like Ross?'

'How long have you known Inspector Ross?' asked Temple.

Forbes considered a moment. 'Let's see – he came to the Yard about 1930, must be fourteen years or more since I first met him. He's a Wimbledon man originally – started in the Force there – then went to Liverpool. Did rather well with those Lascar murder cases at Bootle.'

'How old is he?'

'I looked that up yesterday. He's forty-seven.'

'Married?'

'Yes.'

'You don't know anything about his private life?'

Forbes shook his head. 'No, he's rather secretive in that direction. Likes to keep to himself when he's away from the office.' He lit one of his own cigars.

'Better relax for a little longer before you go to the Yard, Sir Graham,' Temple advised. He turned to Steve.

'I'm going to see Sir Felix this morning,' he told her. 'I'll be back about twelve. If I should be a little late, keep Storey here if you possibly can.'

'All right, darling,' Steve agreed.

'And talking of Sir Felix,' said Forbes, 'I see the papers are still kicking up a fine old fuss.'

'It'll die down,' Temple assured him. 'The papers can't afford to flog a dead horse – even when it comes to life!'

Forbes frowned.

'I wish you'd argue that out with the Home Secretary. I had an unpleasant five minutes on the telephone with him last night. Seems one or two M.P.s have threatened to ask a question about Scotland Yard's unorthodox methods.'

'Why not remind him that every question asked by an M.P. costs the country five pounds?' laughed Temple.

'H'm ... well, as long as we get results,' grunted Forbes, rather dubiously. 'Now, what about this letter to Serflane? I gather you're inclined to take it seriously.'

'That's so, Sir Graham. We shall have to lay our plans very carefully – and moreover the details must be kept secret.'

Forbes sat for a couple of minutes with a far-away look in his eyes as if he were deliberating on a plan of campaign. Suddenly, he sat up.

'I must be off,' he decided, briskly, rising from his chair. 'I've a devil of a day in front of me, mapping out this business. I'll let you know about tonight's arrangements later.'

Forbes moved towards the door a trifle uncertainly, then paused and inquired: 'By the way, where is Sir Felix? You never told me.'

'He's staying at The Clockwise – you know – the night club.'

'The Clockwise?' echoed Forbes in complete amazement. 'Not Maisie Delaway's place?'

'Exactly.'

'Good heavens,' Forbes chuckled. 'We should never have found him in a thousand years!'

The humorous side of the situation seemed to strike the Chief Commissioner, who had always been inclined to take rather an exaggerated view of the risqué qualities of Maisie's entertainment.

'It must be quite an experience for the old boy,' he ruminated, with a wintry smile.

A night club in the cold, hard light of morning is hardly an edifying spectacle, and one that would probably alienate at least fifty per cent of its patrons. The Clockwise proved no exception to this rule when Temple strolled in just after eleven a.m.

The tables had not been cleared, there were many dejected-looking streamers straggling across the room – the previous night had been a gala night – two ancient cleaners were struggling to restore some order from chaos, and in a distant corner four very tired dancers were rehearsing a new routine to a staccato piano accompaniment. Time and again, they repeated the same break until they performed like automata.

Temple went through the dance hall into the office, where he found Gus laboriously counting a huge pile of bank notes and a heap of silver in an audible voice. He looked up suspiciously as the door opened, then smiled expansively as he recognised his visitor.

'Why hello Mr. Temple, this is a surprise.' He pushed the notes aside as if he were glad of an excuse to postpone his calculations.

'Where's Maisie?' asked Temple, having acknowledged his greeting.

'Maybe she's up – maybe not. It's early for her,' said Gus. 'Want to see her?'

'If possible.'

Gus pressed a button and when a diminutive page appeared, sent him to find Maisie. Then he resumed his counting with a sigh.

'You won't mind if I finish this?' he asked Temple. 'I like to get it round to the bank before twelve if I can.'

Temple nodded and perched on the arm of a chair.

When Maisie arrived, Gus showed them into a little private sitting-room behind the office.

She accepted a cigarette, sank into a chair, and placed a pair of neatly slippered feet on another chair.

'Well, Paul,' she smiled, 'what's the trouble?'

'No trouble, Maisie,' he assured her pleasantly. 'I just called in to see your guest. How is he?'

The humorous eyes twinkled.

'Oh, he's fine. Still the perfect gentleman, and no trouble at all. He's kind of getting to like the place – shouldn't wonder if he became a regular customer. He's broad-minded too – thinks my song about the two elephants is just cute – though he says it couldn't have happened with real elephants.'

She paused, and a thoughtful expression flitted across her well-moulded features.

'Say, Paul, why didn't you put me wise to this Egyptology? I believe there may be something to it.'

Temple laughed. 'You've plenty of time before you to explore all the mysteries of the Pharaohs.'

She tossed her head.

'You can laugh, Mr. Temple, M.A., but Sir Felix has as good as promised to take me on his next little trip, believe it or not.'

'I must put a stop to this,' Temple rallied her. 'We can't have our experts diverted from their excavations by glamorous red-heads.'

'Says you!' retorted the red-head in question with a grimace.

'Where is the old boy?' asked Temple.

'He's in the same room – want to see him now?'

183

She jumped to her feet. They found Gus had left the outer office, presumably to deposit his precious burden at the bank. With his hand on the door-handle, Temple paused. Having made certain there was no one within earshot, he murmured: 'Before I forget, Maisie, I want you to try and find out something for me about a girl named Lydia Staines. She was a dancer; went to America about 1929 and worked at the Miami Club on Forty-Second Street for some months.'

Maisie puckered her lips thoughtfully.

'The Miami? That was Harry Van Delson's place in those days,' she called. 'Looks like you might be in luck ...'

'Why?'

'Harry's over here – on the Sanderson Commission.'

'The point is, would he know anything about Lydia Staines?' said Temple.

'When it comes to dames, Harry's got all the telephone numbers,' she informed him with her expansive smile.

'Yes, but have you got his phone number?'

'No,' said Maisie, 'but he's got mine!'

'And who can blame him?'

She tossed the celebrated mane of titian curls. 'I guess I'll run him to earth before the day's out,' she asserted confidently.

They parted at Sir Felix's door.

When Temple entered, the Egyptologist seemed to be doing his best to pacify a distinctly irate Mrs. Clarence.

'It's no use arguing, Sir Felix,' came the rich, penetrating voice, 'you'll get that liver trouble again, stopping in a harum-scarum place like this. Why, just as I came in, I saw a lot of young hussies with nothing on but ... well, you're coming home!'

Mrs. Clarence thumped her substantial umbrella on the floor to emphasise her argument. Sir Felix only smiled as if he were enjoying some secret joke.

'Here's Mr. Temple. He'll answer all your questions, Mrs. Clarence.'

Temple came in and closed the door.

'Hello, Sir Felix. Hello, Mrs. Clarence, what's the trouble?'

'Trouble enough, if you ask me, Mr. Temple,' replied the good lady indignantly. 'This is no place to bring the likes of Sir Felix to – and I'd say the same to the King himself.'

'That's all right, Mrs. Clarence,' the detective reassured her. 'Sir Felix hasn't got to stay here any longer. You can go now, just as soon as you're ready, Sir Felix.'

'Well, I hope that will set Mrs. Clarence's mind at rest,' said Reybourn, faintly amused. 'By gad, some people are going to get a surprise when they find I'm alive and kicking. I hear they'd nominated my successor on the committee at the Institute of Egyptologists.'

'They soon cancelled that, Sir Felix, thanks to Mrs. Clarence,' said Temple meaningly.

'Eh? I don't quite follow you.'

'I'm afraid Mrs. Clarence has disapproved of this scheme right from the start. Furthermore, she felt it her duty to put a stop to it, in the interests of your liver, Sir Felix.'

'I still don't understand.'

'Mrs. Clarence has a young nephew named Ernest Wingby, who is a copy boy on the *Morning Express*,' proceeded Temple evenly. 'A very ambitious lad is young Ernie, he wants to be a reporter. And his idol is a certain Jimmy Fane, the *Express*'s star reporter. Young Ernie tries to copy every original turn of phrase that Jimmy ever used, and I must say he does it very well. In fact, he did it well enough to fool the chief sub, and that's saying a lot.'

'Yes, but how—'

'Mrs. Clarence gave her nephew the story of your faked accident,' announced Temple calmly.

The buxom lady closed her lips in a firm line, and did not attempt to deny the accusation.

'Young Ernie knew very well that the news editor wouldn't let him handle a story like that, and would only send a reporter out on the job. But if the story came from the redoubtable Jimmy Fane, that would be different. So Ernie faked his idol's initials – and hoped that the news editor would relent when he found he'd landed a real scoop.'

Temple shook a warning finger at Mrs. Clarence.

'It was very naughty of you, Mrs. Clarence. I've had to waste a couple of valuable hours making all these inquiries round at the *Morning Express* office. And time is very valuable just now.'

But Mrs. Clarence was quite unrepentant.

'I never could understand why Sir Felix had to go hiding and pretending he was dead,' she declared stoutly. 'A lot of nonsense, if you ask me!'

Reybourn smiled in some amusement. 'It was Temple's idea, not mine,' he reminded her.

'And what about it?' she persisted. 'What was the good of it all?'

'It served a very useful purpose, although you nearly ruined our plans,' said Temple quietly. 'In fact, it was a vital necessity.'

Reybourn looked up quickly.

'What do you mean, Mr. Temple?'

'I mean,' replied Temple, deliberately, 'that beyond any shadow of doubt, I now know who is The Marquis.'

*

186

Temple found Roger Storey in the drawing-room animatedly discussing a recent play with Steve.

'I'm awfully sorry I'm late, Storey,' he apologised. 'Have we any sherry, Steve?'

'Sorry,' said Steve.

'Then mix me a gin and tonic, darling.'

When she had gone to get a fresh bottle of gin, Temple turned to Storey.

'Well, anything happen last night?'

'Nothing very much, I'm afraid,' replied Roger, who was wearing a very expensive Raglan coat.

'You managed to find him all right?'

'Yes, I picked up Ross at Wimbledon, then followed him to a house in Stepney. Apparently, he has a married sister there.'

'How long did he stay?'

'About an hour and a half. I was nearly frozen waiting for him to come out. On the way back to Wimbledon, he popped into a Lyons' cafe and had a meal. Incidentally, I've got a feeling he spotted me. He's rather shrewd, you know.'

'Yes,' said Temple thoughtfully, 'he's shrewd all right.'

At that moment, Steve came in with his drink. He took a sip, then asked: 'Did you tell Storey about that letter, Steve? The one Sir Graham mentioned?'

Steve shook her head. 'We were so busy discussing the new play at the Lyric.'

'What was this letter?' put in Storey, quite eagerly. Temple placed his glass on the table.

'Apparently, your friend Serflane has received a second communication from The Marquis. I'm surprised he hasn't been in touch with you about it.'

Roger appeared quite startled.

'They did tell me there were several telephone calls from a man who would leave no name or message – that was when I was out trailing Ross,' he told them. 'But I thought that business was just a rag when it fizzed out. I took it for granted that it was somebody calling himself The Marquis for a lark.'

Temple sipped his gin and tonic appreciatively.

'On the contrary,' he declared, 'The Marquis has promised to appear in person tonight at eight o'clock in the lounge of the October Hotel, Kensington.'

Roger's amazement grew. 'I say, Temple – you're pulling my leg,' he protested.

'Not at all,' replied Temple quietly.

'But damn it, The Marquis wouldn't walk straight into that hotel with his eyes open.'

'Why not?' asked Temple mildly. 'If he thought that Serflane was the only person likely to be there, he wouldn't be taking much of a risk. Particularly for a return of seven thousand pounds.'

'Or even if there were a risk,' put in Steve, 'he might be one of these people who enjoy that sort of thing.'

She was interrupted by the telephone. Temple put down his glass and went over to the instrument. It was a call from Sir Graham Forbes, who detailed the night's programme in some detail. While he was still talking, Temple felt a touch on his elbow, and Roger whispered: 'Ask him if I can come with you tonight.'

There was a look of such urgent appeal in his eyes that Temple nodded and spoke into the receiver.

'Sir Graham, Storey's here. Yes, he's very keen to come along.'

There was the sound of a small explosion in the earpiece.

'All right, Sir Graham,' said Temple, soothingly, 'I'll guar-antee he won't be a nuisance – yes, I'll make him my personal responsibility! Goodbye!'

Meticulously, he replaced the receiver, then turned to Roger.

'He'll be here soon after seven, just to make sure of the layout, so perhaps you'll join us then. I understand Ross will be in the party, so you can keep him under observation.'

'Right,' said Roger with alacrity, as he collected his hat. 'I'd better be off now. I have a lunch appointment, and after that I can pick up Ross at the Yard. He leaves there about two o'clock this week …'

'No,' Temple decided, 'leave Ross alone for this afternoon at any rate. I happen to know he'll be busy checking up some reports at Bow Street.'

Storey fingered his hat rather uncomfortably.

'I say, Temple, you don't seriously suspect Ross, do you? I mean … well, you might just as well suspect Superintendent Bradley.'

'I do,' retorted Temple, with emphasis. 'As I told you before, I suspect everyone. I have a highly suspicious nature, haven't I, Steve?'

'Yes, I think that would be an accurate description,' decided Steve.

Temple took a gulp at his drink and pulled a wry face.

'M'm, and I suspect that there wasn't much gin in this to start with!'

When Storey had gone, Temple opened his wallet and handed Steve a green slip of paper.

'Before I forget, Steve,' he said, in a business-like tone, 'here's your ticket for tonight.'

'What ticket?' asked Steve, mystified.

'For the theatre, darling. You said you wanted to see the show at the Savoy.'

'But I can't go there tonight,' she interrupted.

'Why ever not?'

'Because,' she announced, decisively, 'I'm coming with you to Kensington.'

'Oh, no, you're not!' snapped Temple.

Her eyes widened. 'Darling, you're not serious,' she protested with an injured air.

'Perfectly serious!'

With some reluctance, she took the ticket and regarded it dubiously.

He sat down at a small table and made some notes in the small black book he always carried. Steve lit a cigarette and fidgeted about the room, moving a vase here and an ornament there. At last she asked:

'Paul, what's going to happen at the hotel tonight?'

He shook his head.

'Your guess is as good as mine,' he replied, gravely. 'But I have an idea it will be calculated to upset even the most hardened lady reporter.' He finished off his drink, and put a hand on her shoulder.

'Take my word for it, darling, you'll be much more comfortable at the theatre.'

CHAPTER XVIII

The October Hotel

KENSINGTON after dark presented a slightly sinister aspect to Temple's imagination. What tragedies, he reflected, were being enacted behind those gaunt, moribund Victorian front-ages, with their high windows, massive porches and peeling plaster? Road after road took on a similarity that was almost alarming. Temple often wondered how its inhabitants found their way back to the right house amid those arid plains of masonry. On the surface, it was all so highly respectable, even genteel.

But the October Hotel was making a bold effort to escape from the Kensington tradition and to cater for the youth of today. Particularly the well-endowed youth. It had been rebuilt in bright red bricks on the site of an ancient hostelry formerly known as The Bear and Staff. Its windows were squat; its doors chromium-plated; its furniture upholstered in striking red leather. Its barmaids, without exception, were platinum blondes of a simply dazzling quality. The hotel had few regular guests of the *en pension* type so favoured by its local competitors. The October Hotel made its money from the two hundred per cent profit on short drinks served to the younger generation, who made a lot of noise, but emptied their pockets without a thought for the morrow. Just lately, the hotel's reputation had been in question once or twice, but so far the police had nothing definitely against the management.

When the police car drew up outside, they could hear an automatic gramophone blaring noisily, and there were gusts of high-pitched laughter. Before starting out, the familiar blue Police sign had been removed from this car and all the others which followed.

'Shall we go in?' asked Forbes, who was impatient to ascertain the lie of the land.

'No, let's wait here for a little while,' decided Temple, lighting a cigarette.

'All right,' agreed Forbes, with some reluctance, as the driver switched off his engine. 'Keep her warm, Johnson,' he advised, 'we might want to get off the mark with a rush.'

'Very good sir,' nodded the driver.

'Wasn't Storey supposed to be coming along?' asked Forbes, presently.

'Yes, he phoned to say he couldn't meet us at the flat, but he'd come straight on. He'll be along presently,' said Temple.

'H'm,' grunted Forbes, without much enthusiasm, 'I think we can manage without him. Where's Steve this evening?'

'She's gone to the theatre.'

'Just as well,' agreed Forbes. 'Shouldn't be surprised if we had a rough house. I've got a feeling that The Marquis is going to force the issue tonight.'

They were silent for a few moments, each brooding upon the train of events which the night would bring forth.

'Careful with that cigarette,' advised Forbes suddenly, when the glow lit up the inside of the saloon. 'We don't want to advertise ourselves any more than we can help. Never know who might be on the lookout for us. The fellow's bound to take precautions, and pretty thorough ones too, if his previous jobs are any indication.'

A figure loomed in the darkness, and exchanged a word with the driver.

'Who's that?' demanded Forbes, sharply.

'Sergeant O'Brien, sir,' said the man outside in a hearty Irish accent.

'Anything to report?' asked Forbes.

'Yes sir.'

'Better get inside the car for a minute,' suggested Forbes, opening the door.

The bulky form of Sergeant O'Brien made its presence felt in the back seat.

'I've been making a few inquiries, sir,' he announced, expansively, 'and, would ye believe it, the hall porter at this place is a fellow named Bertram Carter.'

'The name's familiar,' murmured Temple.

'Yes,' said Forbes swiftly, for he possessed a remarkable memory for names of men with a criminal record. 'There was a Bertram Carter in that big arson case at Birkenhead four years ago.'

'That's the man, sir,' assented O'Brien. 'He was only one of the stooges, as you might say, in that case, as far as we could prove, so he got off with a couple of years penal. I 'phoned the Records Department and they checked up on him.'

A torch flashed suddenly near the kerbside.

'Who the devil's that?' snapped Forbes, irritably. Then he recognised the stocky form. 'Oh, it's you, Bradley.' He lowered the window, and Bradley's head appeared inside.

'Have you seen O'Brien, sir?'

'Yes, he's in here.' Forbes turned to O'Brien. 'Is that all you have to report, Sergeant?'

'That's all, sir,' O'Brien heartily assured him.

'All right, you can go.' O'Brien clambered heavily out of the car and joined Bradley on the pavement.

'Turner's waiting for you,' the Superintendent told him. 'Know where he is?'

'Yes, sir.'

'All right, you've got your orders. And mind you keep your eyes skinned.' O'Brien saluted and disappeared into the darkness.

Bradley leaned in through the open window on Forbes' side, and spoke in a low voice.

'Did O'Brien tell you about the hall porter?' he asked.

'Yes,' said Forbes. 'What d'you make of it?'

'I don't like it at all,' Bradley admitted. 'He's a dangerous devil. Arson seems to have an attraction for him. That was the fourth case he's been mixed up with, but we've never been able to pin anything really definite on him. A couple of hundred years back he'd have been hanged right off, and a good riddance if you ask me.' He relapsed into a gloomy silence, for Bradley was a disappointed man since he had just failed to make Lannie Dukes reveal the identity of The Marquis. Moreover, he was not altogether looking forward to the inquest on Dukes, for he was the only witness of the death, and would be called upon to answer some extremely pertinent questions, if he knew anything about that particular South London coroner.

'What time will Ross be here?' asked Temple, who had not spoken for some minutes.

'Oh, I forgot to tell you,' said Forbes. 'We overlooked the fact that it's his night off. He left Bow Street about four o'clock, didn't he, Bradley?'

'Yes sir. I rang him at four fifteen, and he'd just gone.'

A moon began to rise behind a heavy black cloud, and a chilly east wind swept along the street. The Superintendent shivered and turned up his coat collar.

'How many men have you got on the job now, Bradley?' asked Forbes.

'All the entrances are well-covered, sir,' Bradley assured him. 'Nothing to worry about there.'

The moon came from behind the cloud for a moment or two, then vanished again.

'If you'll excuse me, sir, I'll go and make the round now,' said Bradley, gripping the heavy automatic which lay snugly in his overcoat pocket. With a leisurely tread he moved towards the back entrance of the hotel.

Barely two minutes elapsed when there was a sound of running footsteps, and Sir Graham, who had just raised the window, lowered it again rapidly.

'Stand by, Johnson,' he snapped, peering in the direction of the footsteps. He was about to open the door when he relaxed and said in a disappointed tone: 'Oh, it's you, Storey, I might have known it wasn't one of our men rushing about like that.'

Storey had apparently run some little distance, for he was quite out of breath. He wore no hat, and his hair had been ruffled by the wind, as Temple revealed when he ignited his lighter to start another cigarette.

'Sorry I didn't get to your place, Temple,' panted Roger, 'but Ross passed me in a car when I was on the way there. I jumped into a taxi right away and followed him – I felt somehow he was up to something, and I was right.' He paused to regain his breath.

'Then where the devil is Ross now?' demanded Forbes suspiciously.

'He's here, sir. He drove up the side entrance, parked his car and—'

He was interrupted by several police whistles and the sound of excited voices. Some sort of struggle was obviously taking place not far away. Without any further ado, Forbes and Temple rushed in the direction of the noises. They found Ross struggling in the grip of O'Brien and a plain clothes detective.

'Take your hands off me!' Ross was shouting.

'Easy there, sir,' said O'Brien apologetically, his honest Irish features a trifle bewildered, but quite determined. 'I'm sorry, Mr. Ross, but my orders are to stop everybody at this entrance, even if it's the King himself!'

'To hell with your orders!' stormed Ross. 'I'm giving you orders, and you'll obey them or lose your stripes!'

'I've got my orders from the Superintendent,' persisted O'Brien doggedly, as there was a sound of footsteps, and men converged on them from two different directions. A moment later, Forbes and Temple arrived.

'What's wrong, O'Brien?' demanded Forbes, flashing his torch on the group.

'I'll tell you what's wrong,' cried Ross, struggling to free himself of the sergeant's grip. 'By God, if you think—'

'You're under arrest, Ross,' snapped Forbes, curtly. 'And I warn you that anything you say will—'

A noisy clanging of a fire alarm at the back of the hotel completely drowned his voice.

'Good God!' cried Storey, who had come up behind them. 'Look!'

They all turned and stared in the direction of his pointing finger. On the top floor of the hotel they saw an ominous glow flickering behind two of the windows. Even as they watched, the curtains at one window caught fire. The alarm bell continued its deafening clangour, and people began running in all directions, rendering it quite hopeless for the police on duty to obey their instructions in the face of this confusion.

'Take Ross back to the car, Sergeant,' ordered Forbes briskly, and as O'Brien and his colleague made to obey, Ross started to struggle again. Realising that the Inspector had reached a certain pitch of desperation, and was likely to commit some action he might later regret, Temple stepped forward and confronted Ross abruptly.

'Don't be a damn fool,' he said. 'Go back to the car.'

Ross snarled some indistinct reply.

Temple put a hand on his shoulder.

'Go back to the car, Inspector. When I get a chance I'll tell you more about Lydia Staines. All that need concern you now is the fact that she's dead – died on October the ninth, nineteen thirty-five.'

Ross stood transfixed, unable to make any reply.

'Now for heaven's sake go and sit in the car,' urged Temple. 'I'll talk to you later.'

Like a man in a dream, Ross turned and accompanied O'Brien.

'Who the devil is Lydia Staines?' growled Forbes, as they moved towards the front of the hotel.

'It's a longish story, Sir Graham, and there's no time now,' was the reply. 'Let's get round the other side if we can and see what's going on.'

A fire engine came rattling down the street and pulled up with screeching brakes. By now, the roof had caught fire, and without any delay the escapes began to rear their gaunt framework towards the blaze. There was a little delay in locating the nearest street hydrant, but this was soon connected to the snakelike coils of hosepipes.

'Looks as if it's getting out of control,' commented Forbes, shouting instructions to his men to keep a clear space free of spectators. At that moment, a huge piece of masonry detached itself from the gable and came hurtling downwards, to fall only a few yards away.

'Nasty business altogether,' said Temple, as they walked round to the yard of the hotel. Another fire brigade arrived and feverishly began operations.

They came up to one of Forbes' men who was busily pushing back a fair-sized crowd of people who were flocking from the nearby houses.

'What's going on round here, Turner?' asked Sir Graham.

'Things are serious, sir,' panted Turner. 'Several people trapped on the third floor! The fire seems to have been started in two or three places simultaneously and one or two folks have panicked …'

Temple and Forbes looked at each other and formulated the same thought. Arson!

Forbes was the first to act.

'Keep a sharp look-out for that hall porter, Turner. You know the fellow I mean?'

'Yes sir, Superintendent Bradley passed the word round. But the man seems to have disappeared.'

'If you find him, be sure to hold him.'

'Yes sir.' Turner resumed his unpleasant task.

By this time, the fire had penetrated the outer walls, and the fierce jets of flame illuminated the surroundings for some distance. In this strange glare they distinguished Bradley rushing round as if he were searching for someone.

'Bradley!' called Forbes sharply. 'What's the matter?'

The Superintendent came running across and recognised Temple with some relief.

'Thank heaven I've found you!' he gasped.

'But I've been here all the time,' said Temple. 'Anything wrong?'

'I – I thought you told me Mrs. Temple was at the theatre,' panted Bradley.

'So she is.'

Bradley gulped but did not speak for a moment. Temple noticed his distracted expression, and seized his arm.

'Bradley! What is it?'

Bradley managed to speak at length, slowly and mechanically, like a man emerging from an anaesthetic.

'She's in the hotel,' he said. 'We passed her in ten minutes before the fire broke out.'

For a second the noise, confusion and glare of the fire seemed to whirl through Temple's head like a deafening molten cataract. He felt Forbes take hold of his elbow and draw him away from the others, barking an abrupt order to Bradley as he did so.

'Let's move round to the back – we can get more of the layout from there,' said Forbes. 'Don't get alarmed, Temple. The escapes are all fixed now, and there's a good pressure of water. We'll manage to get everyone out without much trouble.'

He led the way along a narrow alley, and presently they came into a partly covered yard. Here, they found Hart and Banks fully occupied in keeping order among the stream of staff and customers who rushed in and out of the hotel, carrying all sorts of packages and cases, which were dumped in a huge pile at the end of the yard.

Forbes had some difficulty in restraining Temple from dashing into the hotel, and it was only a sudden blast of heat from the fire that deterred him. Still grasping Temple's arm firmly, Forbes stepped back a few paces and surveyed the side of the building. Smoke was pouring out of the windows of the middle floor now, and there was a reflected glare on some of the windows beneath. Just below that, Forbes suddenly saw a door thrust open with considerable force, as if it had stuck and then wrenched outwards. His grip on Temple's arm tightened.

'Temple! It's Steve!'

Temple looked and saw Steve step out on to the small ironwork landing, and in a second she was calmly descending the hotel fire-escape which no one else had apparently thought of using.

'Thank God!' sighed Temple in a relieved voice. 'I hope that stair will hold.'

'It's iron – riveted to the walls,' Sir Graham reassured him.

'But the walls! It must be a furnace inside, suppose they ...'

But before he could speculate any further, Steve was negotiating the last flight of steps and waving to them cheerfully. Temple ran to meet her and almost carried her down the last few stairs.

'Hello darling,' said Steve casually, pulling her hat an inch forward,

'Steve, you little devil!' cried Temple, setting her on her feet. Steve opened her bag, took out a mirror, and by the glare of the fire removed a couple of smuts from her face.

'Of course, this *would* happen,' she murmured. 'Just as I was getting on the trail of—' She stopped and exclaimed anxiously: 'Why, Paul, you look ill. You're as white as a sheet!'

'By Timothy, I feel even whiter!' retorted her husband. 'Dashing into burning buildings to save damsels in distress – at my time of life!'

'You didn't dash into the building,' Steve pointed out, reasonably.

'Well, I was going to!'

'I'm not so sure.'

'Come to think of it,' smiled Temple, who had now regained a certain amount of composure, 'I'm not so sure myself!'

'The only one who seems to be positive is me,' said Forbes, grimly. 'I had a devil of a job to hold him back, Steve. You gave us a hell of a scare.'

Three men came rushing towards them with an uncoiling hose. They were obviously in a considerable hurry.

With them was Sergeant Banks, who came towards his chief. 'I'm sorry to be such a nuisance, sir,' he apologised, 'but the firemen want to work here. Could you move a little further back?'

As they turned to go, there was a roar of falling masonry, and a section of the roof came down a few yards away. Amidst the dust and smoke, they managed to find their way back to the car, coughing and rubbing their eyes. When they had settled inside, Forbes looked round.

'Hello, where did they put Ross?' he demanded.

But the cheerful features of Sergeant O'Brien appeared at the window to reassure him.

'I've got Inspector Ross in the next car, sir,' he announced. 'Fellows is with him – but sure he's as quiet as a lamb.'

'All right, O'Brien, report to me again before we start back.'

The sergeant saluted and returned to his car.

After he had gone, Temple turned to Steve.

'Now Steve, what's the big idea? I told you to go to the theatre! I bought you a ticket to go to the theatre! I even offered to buy your mother a ticket!'

'Yes, I know,' smiled Steve imperturbably. 'But I wanted to satisfy my curiosity. Anyhow, I found out something.'

'Indeed?'

'Yes, the hall porter at the hotel is the man who came for me at Pevensey, the one who called himself Morris.'

'Then why didn't you have him arrested? You knew the place was swarming with police.'

'Easier said than done. As soon as he saw I'd recognised him, he dashed upstairs like a flash of lightning. And it was just after that the fire alarm went. So I found out something, even if The Marquis didn't turn up.'

'But The Marquis did turn up,' interposed Temple gently, in a remonstrative tone.

Steve sat up with a jerk. It would be difficult to decide whether she or Sir Graham was the more surprised.

'He did turn up?' queried Forbes, incredulously.

'That's what I said,' murmured Temple, gazing thoughtfully at the fire outside.

'I don't follow you, Paul,' protested Steve in bewilderment. 'I tell you I sat in the lounge for a quarter of an hour and no one …'

'Temple!' interposed Forbes, urgently. 'You mean to say you know who The Marquis really is?'

Temple nodded calmly. 'I do. And what's more, I'll introduce you to him, Sir Graham, at the first suitable opportunity.'

'When?' demanded Forbes bluntly.

Temple considered this for a moment, then announced: 'Tomorrow night. We might even make a party of it, a nice friendly sort of party. Just the people who have been hunting The Marquis, with one or two others, such as—'

'Well?'

'Such as Sir Felix Reybourn, for instance. And of course, Mrs. Clarence. We mustn't forget that good lady. You must meet her, Sir Graham; she has considerable influence with the *Morning Express,*' chuckled Temple. He turned to his wife.

'How d'you feel about it, Steve? Are you equal to the strain of a party?'

'Certainly, darling. Anything you suggest.'

'All right then. There's hardly time to get cards printed, but' – he turned to the Chief Commissioner – 'Mr. and Mrs. Temple request the pleasure of Sir Graham Forbes' presence at an informal party on Wednesday. Cocktails at seven ...' He paused, then added quietly: 'to meet The Marquis.' Noticing Forbes' grim expression, he added with a smile:

'It's all right, Sir Graham. We shan't be playing Murder ... I hope!'

CHAPTER XIX

Introducing The Marquis!

IN a South London police court which was furnished rather like a university lecture room, the coroner looked over his pince-nez at Superintendent Bradley and frowned thoughtfully.

'I suppose we must take your word as to the rather remarkable manner in which the deceased met his death, Superintendent, but I must say that never before in my ten years' experience as a coroner have I encountered a police report which has been so unsatisfactory.'

'I'm sorry, sir,' replied Bradley, in a tone that was almost pugnacious.

'I'm sorry, too, Superintendent!' The coroner scanned his notes and made a small correction. Then he looked up again.

'You tell me that the deceased has a criminal record. How far back does that go?'

'Somewhere about twelve years, sir. I've got his record here, sir, if you'd care to see it.'

Bradley passed over a sheet of paper.

'H'm, yes ...' murmured the coroner as he scrutinised it, 'not exactly a desirable citizen.'

'He'd given us a lot of trouble, sir,' declared Bradley, with some emphasis.

'Quite so. But that unfortunately does not alter the fact that this man was apparently murdered in cold blood.'

'I was there to arrest him,' explained Bradley patiently. 'We had evidence that he was implicated in the cocaine traffic.'

'Then why didn't you take him away immediately?'

'I was giving him a chance to tell me one or two things off the record.'

'Isn't that rather an unorthodox procedure?'

'In this case,' replied Bradley, firmly, 'it was necessary to exploit unorthodox methods. There were certain important issues involved, and I was anxious to save as much time as possible.'

This reply sounded impressive, but served only to whet the general curiosity, and did not satisfy the coroner.

'You must understand, Superintendent, that we are viewing this case from rather different angles,' he insisted. 'I am merely anxious to establish the exact cause of the death of this – er – Lannie Dukes.'

'I told you, sir, he was shot by someone at the door who ...'

'Yes, yes,' interrupted the coroner, testily, 'but you have no proof of that. No witnesses have come forward.' He took off his pince-nez and frowned at Bradley. 'For all we know, Superintendent, it would be just as feasible to say that *you* shot Dukes ...'

'I had no weapon,' replied Bradley, stolidly.

'Yes, I daresay, but we have only your word for that again. You had ample opportunity to dispose of any weapon. Don't misunderstand me, Superintendent,' he added hastily, noting Bradley's change of expression. 'I am only putting forward a theory, which on the face of it is quite as credible as your own statement.'

He polished his pince-nez and replaced them.

'Now, Superintendent, supposing we accept your statement, have you any idea as to who might be likely to shoot this man?'

'Yes sir,' replied Bradley, flatly. 'Since you ask me, there isn't much doubt in my mind that The Marquis shot him.'

'The Marquis?' repeated the coroner. 'Isn't that the gentleman we read so much about in the newspapers?' From his tone of voice he might have been discussing a character in fiction. Master criminals were obviously rather outside his experience.

'That's the man,' said Bradley abruptly, in reply to the question.

'H'm, well, to continue ... what motive do you suggest The Marquis might have for killing this man Dukes?'

'Dukes was a member of his gang, sir,' replied Bradley.

'But surely that's hardly a satisfactory explanation—'

Rather reluctantly, Bradley took a wallet from his pocket and extracted an envelope.

'I would like to produce this letter as evidence of motive, sir. But I must ask that the contents are not published.'

There was a considerable amount of whispering in court as the coroner took the slip of notepaper, and read:

You were clever, Bradley, but not clever enough. I have been watching Lannie for some days in case something like this happened. This time, there was only an opportunity for one shot. Next time may be different.

The Marquis.

*

207

Temple spent the greater part of that morning securing the ingredients for a strange new cocktail, the recipe for which he had brought back from America with him. The ingredients were both numerous and peculiar, and he could not resist mixing a small quantity by way of trial. Steve sampled it dubiously, but decided that it was at least different from any other cocktail she had ever tasted.

After that, Temple spent an hour or so making a number of telephone calls. He also sent a wire to Inspector Ross.

During the afternoon he shut himself in his study, and wrote solidly for nearly three hours, much to the mystification of Steve, who could not suppress a growing feeling of excitement, mingled with intense curiosity. However, when she had made the least tentative attempt to cross-question her husband, he had returned flippant replies or changed the subject with disconcerting ease.

Just before tea, he telephoned The Clockwise and asked for Maisie. When the familiar voice greeted him, he said: 'How would you like to come to a party at my place tonight?'

There was an annoyed imprecation from the other end.

'I'd have loved it, Paul,' she replied in a regretful tone. 'But I guess it's impossible tonight. This is a fine time to ask a girl! Somebody let you down?'

'Certainly not! You see, Maisie, it's one of those last-minute parties. Sir Felix will be there,' he added as an afterthought.

'Don't tempt me!' she cried, 'We've got a special night on here – Freemasons or Elks or some other kids' party. They stipulated that I've got to play hostess, or the deal's off.'

After a little further badinage, he replaced the receiver and went in to tea.

'I have a bit of news for Sir Felix,' he said to Steve, as he stirred his tea. She sat up expectantly.

'Yes darling, what is it?'

'I've decided that I really will start a book about Egypt,' he informed her. And to Steve's annoyance, he still refused to discuss The Marquis.

Sir Felix Reybourn and Mrs. Clarence were the first to arrive, soon after seven. The Egyptologist was quite meticulously dressed in a well-cut lounge suit, and affected a bow tie which made him appear even more distinguished. Mrs. Clarence followed him rather reluctantly, as though she had been brought along against her better judgment. In fact, Steve imagined she heard a muttered protest as Mrs. Clarence handed Pryce her voluminous umbrella, and trailed along the hall in the wake of her employer. When Temple offered her a drink, she immediately refused a cocktail in no uncertain manner, but eventually agreed to 'a nice glass of sherry.' Sir Felix was in a more venturesome mood, and declared himself quite ready to sample the new cocktail.

'M'm ...' he sipped it, thoughtfully. 'What did you say this was called, Temple?'

'Serpent's Tooth,' replied the host, watching him rather anxiously.

Sir Felix shook his head. 'I wouldn't like to take the consequences if it were administered to my serpents,' he declared. 'Still, it's most – er – refreshing – and invigorating. I'm almost tempted to try another.'

Just as Temple was refilling his glass, Roger Storey came in, apparently in a hurry as usual. Temple left Sir Felix to talk to Steve, and went across to offer Storey a drink. Rather to his surprise, he observed that Roger was wearing a suit he had seen before, though there was no mistaking the fact that his blue and white silk tie was brand new.

'A whisky, if I may,' he replied, when asked what he would drink. Then he lowered his voice. 'What's the idea of this party, Temple?'

'Oh, just a sort of celebration,' replied the novelist evasively. 'We're making an announcement later on.'

'I see – one of these anniversary affairs,' concluded Roger with a grin, taking a sip at his whisky. 'You should have told us more about it, and we might have rallied round with gifts.'

'I was afraid that would reduce the attendance,' replied Temple, hastily. 'By the way, have you met Sir Felix Reybourn?'

'Well no,' said Storey, with some hesitation, 'I can't say I have. Heard a lot about him of course ...'

Temple took Roger over and introduced him to Sir Felix, at the same time refilling Mrs. Clarence's glass. That good lady now appeared a little more cheerful, and was relating to Steve with a certain ghoulish satisfaction all the 'goings-on' she had witnessed at The Clockwise.

Ross entered unobtrusively before Pryce could announce him. His manner was quiet and somewhat subdued. He had waited in his office at the Yard all day for a summons from his chief, but none had come. He had varied between moods of uncertainty and extreme depression, and had finally left early, to find Temple's telegram awaiting him at home. It had been quite a pleasantly worded invitation, and one he felt he dared not refuse.

Temple seemed very pleased and just a little surprised to see him.

'Why, hello, Ross,' he called across the room. 'I am glad you managed to get here. You look cold. Have a drink?'

'Thanks, Mr. Temple, I could do with a whisky,' Ross admitted.

'You got my telegram then?' said Temple when he brought the drink.

Ross nodded. 'I thought maybe you wanted to see me alone – about Lydia—'

'Presently,' said Temple, as another arrival was announced. It was Sir Graham Forbes.

'Good evening, Ross,' said his chief pleasantly enough, as if he were greeting an acquaintance at the club.

'Good evening, Sir,' replied Ross respectfully, wondering if and when things would come to a head.

'I've been waiting for you, Sir Graham,' said Temple. 'Whisky and soda?'

'Please.'

Temple busied himself fetching drinks and introducing his guests, and Steve was also kept fully occupied dispensing hospitality. The last arrival was Superintendent Bradley, who seemed both mildly astonished by the number of people and the party atmosphere. Moreover, he was not in a very pleasant mood, having spent rather a trying afternoon at the inquest of the mysterious death of Lannie Dukes. The coroner had thrown more than one strong hint that it was Bradley's job to enlighten him as to the identity of the killer, and that he was falling woefully short of his duty in maintaining a discreet silence on this subject.

Bradley had quite understood that his invitation to Temple's flat was strictly concerned with business.

'I'm not much of a party man, Mr. Temple,' he declared in a gruff voice which contained a note of reproach. However, he accepted a tankard of beer. 'Come to that,' he continued, 'I can't see much call for a party just now.'

'This is business as well as pleasure, Bradley,' Temple gravely assured him. 'And I want you to be on your guard.

I'm telling you quite seriously, anything may happen!'

'Very good, Mr. Temple,' replied Bradley, looking somewhat sceptical nevertheless. At that moment, Pryce came in to announce: 'The drawing-room is quite ready now, madam.'

'Thank you, Pryce,' said Steve, and looked across at her husband expectantly. Temple raised his voice.

'Listen everybody! There's a very pleasant fire in the drawing-room, and a number of very comfortable chairs. I want you all to go in there – take your drinks along – and make yourselves as cosy as possible. I have one or two explanations to make, and it may take some little time.'

The guests eyed each other somewhat dubiously, as if they were being called on to start some strange new game. Their conversation died to a murmur as they made for the door in ones and twos.

When they had settled on the restful green upholstered settees and armchairs in the drawing-room, Temple leaned against a corner of the mantelpiece and faced his audience.

'I expect you are all wondering why I invited you here this evening,' he began. 'Perhaps some of you realise that I had a most particular reason for doing so. Sir Graham, for instance! Last night, outside of the October Hotel, Sir Graham asked me if I knew who The Marquis was, *and I promised to introduce him to The Marquis – tonight!*'

There was a general stir amongst the guests. Bradley casually plunged his hand in the coat pocket where he carried his automatic pistol.

Sir Felix set down his cocktail glass.

'Do you mean that The Marquis is actually coming here tonight?' he asked, in an amazed voice. Temple stooped to poke the fire, then turned, still holding the poker.

'The Marquis is already here, Sir Felix,' he announced, quietly.

'What d'you mean – already here?' demanded Storey swiftly.

Bradley leaned forward in his chair at the side, where he had a good view of everyone.

'Mr. Temple, you don't mean that he's here in this room. Actually one of us!'

'That,' replied Temple placidly, as he carefully replaced the poker, 'is precisely my meaning, Bradley.'

He could not repress a smile at the attitude of mingled alarm and dismay with which some of his guests were regarding each other.

'I know this is bound to upset Sir Felix's liver again,' Mrs. Clarence informed Steve in a loud whisper.

Forbes took a cigar from his pocket, held it to his ear and cut it with great care. 'I think you owe us an explanation, Temple,' he murmured quietly.

'Of course I owe you an explanation, Sir Graham, and I intend to give you one. Suppose we begin at the beginning. Let me, in fact, start with suspect number one! Sir Felix Reybourn!'

Sir Felix nodded approvingly, and cleared his throat.

'As a keen student of crime fiction I am extremely interested, Mr. Temple. Please proceed.'

Temple deliberately enumerated the points in the case against Sir Felix.

'Forty-eight hours before Lady Alice Mapleton was murdered, she paid Sir Felix a visit. Twenty-four hours before the police discovered the body of Carlton Rodgers, he had dined with Sir Felix at his house at St. John's Wood. And the last person to see Myron Harwood alive, on his own admission, was Sir Felix Reybourn. Now, these are the cold, definite, undisputed facts.'

'I quite agree, Mr. Temple,' put in Sir Felix, with a trace of irritation. 'But we have surely covered this ground before.

I gave you the explanations for all those facts, and, as you very readily concurred, if I were The Marquis, I would hardly have drawn attention to myself in such a highly incriminating manner.'

'That's so, Sir Felix,' Temple reassured him. 'As soon as you pointed that out to me, I began to consider the possibility that someone – and whom else but The Marquis? – was deliberately throwing suspicion upon Sir Felix. The theory wasn't very popular, I'm afraid, but I stuck to it.'

Temple paused to light a cigarette.

'Well now, how did we get to hear about Sir Felix?' he continued easily. 'Speaking for myself ...'

'I told you about him,' interrupted Storey quickly. 'It was Rita Cartwright, you remember ...'

'Quite so,' agreed Temple, 'you told us about him, Storey. And that led eventually to Roddy Carson and suspect number two—Inspector Ross.'

Ross's lean features betrayed no sign of emotion, and Temple continued: 'When the body of Roddy Carson was discovered at Forard Glen he had, amongst other things, an envelope in his pocket. On the back of it was scribbled "Sir Felix Reybourn, 492 Maupassant Avenue, St. John's Wood." Now you remember the first thing that struck me about this was the word "Maupassant" being spelt correctly. I knew instinctively that Roddy Carson hadn't written the words. For one thing, the writing didn't tally with the letter he had previously sent Sir Graham. For another, he could hardly spell his own name, let alone the word Maupassant. *Now why were those words written on the back of an envelope, and why was that envelope planted on the body of Roddy Carson?*'

'Presumably to continue to throw suspicion on Sir Felix,' hazarded Bradley, from the depths of his tankard.

'Yes, but that wasn't the only reason. You see, I discovered that the handwriting on the envelope was that of Inspector Ross.'

This caused quite a sensation, but Ross remained quite unperturbed.

'Now what did that mean?' went on Temple. 'As I saw it, it could only mean one of three things. Either Ross was The Marquis, or he was a confederate of The Marquis, or ...'

'Or he was a victim!' supplied Roger Storey, eagerly.

'In other words,' said Forbes, 'Ross was being blackmailed!'

At last Ross betrayed some signs of interest.

'How did you find out, Temple?' he demanded, unable to suppress a note of curiosity in his voice.

'It wasn't easy,' Temple informed him. 'And I had to take Bradley into my confidence. Together, we arranged Sir Felix's accident and "death." The whole country thought he was dead, including The Marquis. This threw a new complexion on the case. If Sir Felix was dead, it meant that The Marquis had to shift suspicion on to someone else for any future crimes.'

'And the obvious choice was Ross!' declared Forbes, grimly.

'That's so. And you know what happened. Ross became our prime suspect almost immediately.'

'Yes, my God, yes!' cried Ross, really aroused by now. 'The day we all thought Sir Felix had been killed I had a note ordering me to write to Serflane, demanding seven thousand pounds in the name of The Marquis.'

'But good God, Ross, why was he blackmailing you?' demanded the Chief Commissioner.

'That's rather a long story,' said Temple. 'Briefly, however, Ross was under the impression that he had committed bigamy, but fortunately for him, by a sheer coincidence, his first wife, Lydia Staines, died in New York a month before his second marriage.'

'Really, this is extremely interesting,' said Sir Felix, who had followed each step of the argument with great care.

'If Ross isn't The Marquis,' put in Storey pertinently, 'who is?'

'Can't you guess?' asked Temple, lightly, blowing out a cloud of smoke.

'No, I'm damned if I can.'

'Look here, Temple,' said Bradley in some irritation, 'if you don't know who The Marquis is, for God's sake say so, and let's get back on the job.'

'But I do know,' said Temple softly, as he stubbed out his cigarette with a decisive gesture. 'Bradley, you remember the lorry that smashed into my car on the embankment?'

'Yes.'

'Why do you think they didn't find the lorry driver?'

'He disappeared,' replied the Superintendent in a puzzled voice. Temple shook his head.

'Oh no! *That's just the point, Bradley. He didn't disappear.*'

'What do you mean?'

'I mean,' replied Temple deliberately, and with sudden emphasis, '*that the lorry was driven by Mr. Storey.*'

'What!'

Roger leapt to his feet.

'Sit down, Storey. There's more to come.' With a gesture Temple silenced him. Then Temple said: 'Why did Storey turn up at the inn at Pevensey just before Slater was killed?'

'You know damn well why I turned up,' snapped Roger. 'To tell you about Sir Felix and—' Temple waved aside his explanation.

'You turned up because you were already in the district, and were frightened of being seen.'

'But what about his car accident with Slater?' asked Forbes.

'Faked,' said Temple, briefly. 'Storey is rather an expert at car accidents. He knew perfectly well what Slater was going to do.'

'That's a lie!' shouted Roger.

'Naturally, if Storey could convince us that attempts were being made on his life, it would distract suspicion from falling on him,' pursued Temple, calmly. 'Again, there was the doped cigarette. Who else could have planted it?'

Storey was on his feet again in an instant, but this time he made a deliberate move towards the door. As he passed a small bureau, he suddenly wrenched open the top drawer and pulled out a small revolver which Temple kept there, and which Storey had apparently discovered on a previous visit.

'Put that gun down, Storey; it isn't loaded,' ordered Temple, making no move.

'Isn't it?' said Storey. He plunged his hand into his coat pocket and produced an automatic. 'Well, *this* one is, Mr. Temple!' He swung round menacingly. 'Would you like me to prove it?'

Without any further ado, he fired at a photograph on the piano. There was a tinkling of glass as the frame toppled over.

'Stand back everybody!' advised Storey, who had now reached the door. 'You Bradley! Put your hands up and move into that corner. And remember if anyone follows me out of this room I shall let them have it!' There was no mistaking the cold fury in his voice.

With his left hand he suddenly pulled the door open, and in less than a second he had vanished. There was an immediate movement towards the door. Temple got there first and opened it cautiously a few inches. Looking over his shoulder, Forbes was just in time to see Storey disappearing through a door at the far end of the hall.

'Where's it lead to?' panted Forbes.

'Emergency exit,' replied Temple. 'It opens on to a flight of stairs up to the roof.'

'Good enough,' snapped Forbes. 'No time to lose. Ross! Bradley! Run down below and get all the men you can to watch the exits right round this block.'

Forbes and Temple rushed in Storey's wake, and as they opened the door of the emergency exit they heard the thud of a wooden trapdoor on to the roof. When they reached the top of the stairs, Temple lifted the trapdoor without much difficulty, and after a moment's hesitation they clambered out. The blackness was not completely dense when their eyes became accustomed to it.

'Can't see anything of him,' whispered Forbes, looking quickly in all directions. 'He might be hiding behind any of these chimneys.'

'No, I think he's out to make a quick getaway,' muttered Temple. They advanced cautiously, moving as quietly and unobtrusively as possible.

'Shall I use my torch?' suggested Forbes.

'Better not,' Temple advised. 'It'll only present him with an easy mark – and he's desperate.'

'Hsst ...' said Forbes suddenly. 'There he is!'

Temple followed his pointing arm, and saw a dark form near the edge of the parapet, some twenty yards away.

'Stay where you are, Temple!' shouted Roger suddenly. 'D'you hear me? Stay where you are! I've got you covered!'

'My God! He's going to jump down on the annexe!' breathed Temple incredulously.

'How far is it?'

'About twenty feet, but it's the restaurant, and they've got a glass roof covered with a blackout sheet!'

'Phew!' whistled Forbes.

'Storey!' Temple called, advancing a pace. 'It's a glass roof! Don't jump!'

'Stay where you are, Temple!' Obviously Storey had decided that the warning was a ruse on Temple's part, for he placed a foot on the parapet, paused a moment, then disappeared.

There was a terrific crash, followed by a desperate shriek.

Temple and Forbes reached the parapet to see a star-shaped hole through which the light was shining. From below there came the sound of shouts and general confusion.

'Well, he didn't fake that accident,' said Forbes, grimly.

At breakfast next morning, Temple had to contend with a further barrage of questions from Steve. For a time, he buried himself behind his paper, and refused to be drawn.

'I say, this is a frightful photograph of Sir Graham in the *Morning Express*,' he chuckled. 'It rather reminds me of Charlie McCarthy.' He continued to read.

'I must say this is a very garbled report of the case,' he commented. 'Not that I begrudge Sir Graham his lion's share of the limelight.'

'Can you wonder he gets it?' said Steve, 'when you won't even tell your own wife how you cleared up the case. If I hadn't told the reporters what little I know, I doubt if your name would have appeared at all.'

Temple laughed and laid down his paper.

'You've been popping questions at me all night like a third-degree expert. I've hardly had a wink of sleep,' he complained with an air of injured innocence. 'I suppose there's no peace until I've satisfied your feminine curiosity. Now, what was it you were so anxious to know?'

Steve considered for a moment.

'Well, in the first place, why did you get Storey to trail Ross?'

'For obvious reasons. I wanted Storey to believe I was under the impression that Ross was The Marquis.'

'Yes, but why did Storey always push himself to the fore? At the beginning, I mean, when he made all those inquiries about The Marquis. He was always here or with Sir Graham.'

Temple pushed his plate aside and lit a cigarette.

'Yes, he was almost brilliant there. He created a part for himself, and he played it very well. He was almost the amateur detective – and who suspects the amateur detective? No one, of course, except himself?'

'You said you suspected everybody,' she reminded him.

'That's because I happen to be a novelist. We authors are a suspicious crowd,' he smiled. 'Next question?'

She wrinkled her forehead.

'Let me see. Oh yes, about Lydia Staines! How did you discover she was dead?'

'Maisie found that out for me. She's pretty good at that sort of research.'

Steve leaned her chin on her hand, and looked at him across the table.

'I must say I can't understand Roger Storey,' she confessed. 'A young man with a good education and apparently considerable private means. What was the motive of all these crimes he committed?'

Temple leaned back in his chair and toyed with his coffee spoon.

'Forbes and I were just about as curious as you are when we searched his flat late last night.'

'What did you find?'

'We found enough to bring us to the conclusion that Storey was a sort of cultured prototype of Jack the Ripper,' announced Temple, deliberately. 'It seems that crime has always fascinated him. He began in a small way when he was at Oxford; stole money and valuables from dons and tutors and contrived to get the blame thrown on to other people. One undergraduate was actually sent down as a result.'

'It sounds incredible,' murmured Steve.

'It was all set out in his diaries,' Temple assured her. 'He kept a very neat record of every crime, with dozens of press cuttings pasted on the opposite pages. When he was at Oxford, he had already collected a considerable number of books on criminology, and obviously the subject became more and more intriguing. I rather suspect that if he had confined his efforts to forging bank notes he could have lived in luxury for the rest of his life.'

'But what about Lady Alice?' Steve reminded him.

'I'm coming to that. Storey decided to go in for dope distribution in a really big way. That's how he came to meet Lady Alice. According to his diaries, she had a very strange effect on him. Up till then, he had not been interested in women, or indeed in any other human being apart from their criminal possibilities. Yet right from their first meeting, he found himself strangely fascinated by her. Indeed, during their engagement, Storey discovered a new and sadistic delight in inflicting a refined form of torture upon his fiancée: at one minute threatening to make public her dope-taking, at the next to withdraw supplies. God knows what minor cruelties he inflicted on the poor girl during those awful months. She dared not tell anyone the whole truth, though her mother found out about the cocaine. Can you wonder that Alice went to Sir Felix Reybourn in desperation when she heard a rumour about that habit-breaking drug he'd brought back from Egypt? It seemed to offer her a last, desperate chance.'

Temple paused.

'I'm afraid Sir Felix didn't tell us quite everything. He is, I find, quite a friend of the Mapleton family and I suppose he was considering their feelings. However, Storey's diary tells the approximate truth, as he extorted it from Alice. It seems that she wouldn't take "no" from Sir Felix about that habit-breaking drug, and to pacify her, Sir Felix told her that he had given it to Harwood. She went to Harwood's house, and Storey followed her there. She confessed practically everything to Harwood, just as she had done to Rodgers on the night he dined with Sir Felix. That meant that three men knew that Lady Alice Mapleton was receiving dope from a criminal source. Either of them might go to the police any day. So Storey planned a series of murders, and' – concluded Temple – 'so far as I can judge, he accomplished the murders in much the same frame of mind that a chess player removes pieces from the board.'

Steve poured out a second cup of coffee and as Temple stirred it, he murmured casually: 'Pity about that photograph of your mother. The one that Storey shattered.'

'Yes, the bullet completely ruined it.'

'I was greatly attached to that picture,' he said, gravely. 'The only glamorous photo we have in the flat.'

'Beast!'

'Anyhow, this was a grand recipe for American coffee your mother gave you. I shall be eternally in her debt,' he admitted, drinking appreciatively. Steve came over and stood by his side.

'Paul, there's something else I want to ask you,' she said seriously.

'You mean about this case?'

'In a way.'

Steve was hesitating in a manner which was quite unfamiliar. She turned her back on him and looked into the fire. At last, she said in a low voice: 'Was Maisie Delaway a *very* old friend of yours?'

Temple could not restrain a huge shout of laughter. When this had subsided, he began to look through his letters.

'I'd quite forgotten this,' he told her, selecting one from the pile. 'It concerns both of us.'

'What is it?'

'An invitation to a wedding.'

'A wedding?'

'Yes, on December 29th, at Marylebone Register Office, Miss Maisie Delaway proposes to take the plunge for the fourth time with ...' He paused, tantalisingly. 'Guess who?'

Steve shook her head helplessly. 'I haven't the least idea. Who is he?'

Paul Temple chuckled.

'The bridegroom will be none other than Sir Felix Reybourn, the eminent Egyptologist!'